PRAISE FOR *WIMM*

Winner, 2016 DEBUT DAGGER, UK Crime Writers' Association
Winner, 2018 DEBUT FICTION AWARD, Indie Book Awards
Shortlisted, 2018 BEST DEBUT CRIME, Ned Kelly Awards
Shortlisted, 2018 LITERARY FICTION BOOK OF THE
YEAR, Australian Book Industry Awards
Shortlisted, 2018 MATT RICHELL AWARD FOR NEW
WRITER OF THE YEAR, Australian Book Industry Awards

'The reader is in the hands of a master storyteller . . .
This is literary crime fiction at its best'
Books+Publishing

'Very little fiction is as emotionally true as this. *Wimmera* is a
dark and disturbing story from a substantial new talent'
Saturday Paper

'What makes *Wimmera* so effective, and original, is the pacing
and restraint'
Sydney Morning Herald

'Subtle and devastating.
The novel crackles with suspense and dread'
Australian Book Review

'*Wimmera* makes excellent use of atmospheric rural Australia to
weave a gothic story with a strongly rooted sense of place'
Herald Sun

PRAISE FOR *THE RIP*

Longlisted, 2019 BEST FICTION, Ned Kelly Awards
Longlisted, 2020 FICTION AWARD, Indie Book Awards

'*The Rip* pulled me into its unpredictable waters, and refused to
let go; authentic, heartfelt . . . and original'
SOFIE LAGUNA

'A superb book – beautifully conceived, masterfully executed.
A winner'
CHRIS HAMMER

'[an] accomplished second novel that certainly
live[s] up to the promise of the first'
Sydney Morning Herald

'stripped-back and intimate . . . there's no doubting the skill with
which Brandi ratchets up the tension'
Weekend Australian

'a fast-paced crime novel full of dread and suspense'
Herald Sun

'another tension builder'
Courier Mail

'What held me close in this novel was not the idea of a hidden
population of drifters and addicts, but the writer's reassurance
that dignity and small kindnesses have a place in that world'
JOCK SERONG

PRAISE FOR *THE OTHERS*

SOUTHERN AURORA

MARK BRANDI

hachette
AUSTRALIA

This project has been assisted by the Australian Government through the Australia Council, its arts funding and advisory body.

 This project is supported by the Victorian Government through Creative Victoria.

This manuscript was first developed as part of the HARDCOPY Program at MARION (formerly ACT Writers).

Published in Australia and New Zealand in 2023
by Hachette Australia
(an imprint of Hachette Australia Pty Limited)
Gadigal Country, Level 17, 207 Kent Street, Sydney, NSW 2000
www.hachette.com.au

Hachette Australia acknowledges and pays our respects to the past, present and future Traditional Owners and Custodians of Country throughout Australia and recognises the continuation of cultural, spiritual and educational practices of Aboriginal and Torres Strait Islander peoples. Our head office is located on the lands of the Gadigal people of the Eora Nation.

 A catalogue record for this book is available from the National Library of Australia

ISBN: 978 0 7336 4932 5 (paperback)

Cover design by Christabella Designs
Cover photographs courtesy of Trevillion
Author photograph courtesy of Georgia Dodds
Typeset in 12.25/18.25 pt Adobe Garamond Pro by Bookhouse, Sydney
Printed and bound in Great Britain by Clays Ltd, Elcograf S.p.A.

For my mum

PROLOGUE

Tippy was a super dog. Best one we ever had.

A kelpie, black as ink with a white patch on his chest. Nothing and no one could stop him. Best dog in town. Easy.

Only thing was, sometimes he liked to run away.

Mick reckoned he was going out rooting, because it'd mostly happen in spring and he'd usually be gone for a couple of days at least. Sometimes he'd come back with long welts across his back, like someone had given him a whipping.

After the fourth or fifth time, Mick reckoned we couldn't have him loose in the backyard anymore, so he chained him to the water bowl, with a padlock and everything. Tippy's water bowl wasn't a normal one like people get from the shops. It was this enormous cast-iron pot we scavved from the tip. Really heavy.

We found him miles away, dragging that cast-iron pot along the road like a complete mental case. He must've been desperate for a root, to drag it all that way. It still had some water in it, so he could have a drink when he got tired. That's what Mick said.

Mick's my older brother, and he has an opinion on most things, even if he's wrong sometimes. Mick's real name is Michael, but everyone calls him Mick, even Mum. He really cracks it if you call him Michael.

Only Nan called him that. She's the only one who could get away with it. She's the one who called me Jimmy too. My real name's Jim, but it was Jimmy that stuck. Mum says I was named after Jim Hawkins in *Treasure Island*, which is a movie and a book. She says she's only seen the movie, though.

When the water bowl didn't work, Mick chained Tippy to the fence out back. He didn't like it much. He barked a lot. Then he'd go quiet for a bit. Then he'd start up barking again.

I realised later that the quiet time must have been when he was thinking about what he was gonna do. Planning it all out.

So when I took him off the chain to put him in Mick's car, Tippy took off like a shot. It was like he thought, *You can stuff that for a joke, I'm not going back on that chain again!* and he bolted down the side of the house and out into the street like a rocket. Mick yelled out and we all ran after him. Even Mum and Sam. Sam's my younger brother.

But there was no catching Tippy. He was way too fast and way too smart for us.

Someone caught him in the end, though.

It was about a week later when Mick found him. I remember because Mum was at work and Mick came home with these big eyes that didn't blink for ages.

Then he said, 'Tippy's dead.' Just like that.

I held in my tears, swallowed them down. I tried to be tough because otherwise Mick would say I was being a sook. I knew it was my fault Tippy had got away, and I felt sick in my guts. I asked what happened.

He shrugged. 'Someone shot him.'

'Really?'

'Yep. I found him near the back road to the tip. He's still there.'

I asked Mick to take me, but he reckoned he was too busy because he had to go pick up his Pacer from the mechanics. Then I begged him. So he said okay, but made me promise to make his bed for the rest of the year. That turned out to be a pretty good deal, because he went to jail not long after.

•

The tip is a fair way out of town. There's a couple of good ways to get there, but the quickest on the bikes is the fire access road, which is out near the rifle range.

I'm always a bit scared going past the rifle range. Mick told me once that some kid got hit by a stray bullet that went right through his heart. 'Dead before he hit the ground,' he said. That story was almost definitely bullshit, but it still made me nervous.

Mick rode about twenty metres ahead and was going pretty quick, even with the shovel across his handlebars. The shovel was so we could bury Tippy properly. I'd asked him if we could take it.

Mick never liked it if I rode too close. It was the same if we walked somewhere, I always had to stay a bit behind. I didn't mind. He had a much faster bike anyway, a cruiser. He got it from one of his mates. Mine's just a BMX and it's a few years old and too small for me. Mick put the seat up as far as it could go, but it's still too small.

We got to the start of the fire access road. The road wound through the bush, all loose gravel and dust. I gritted my teeth and listened out for the crack of a gun. I thought for sure I was gonna get shot. Or maybe Mick would get shot, and then it would be my fault for making him take me, and Mum would never forgive me. Even if Mick upsets her sometimes, I know she really loves him. I could almost see her face if I had to tell her Mick was dead. It'd be pretty awful.

I slowed down a bit because I thought it was better if we rode further apart, so we'd be a harder target. But then I remembered it was a stray bullet that killed that kid, so it wouldn't make any difference.

Mick stopped his bike and waited for me to catch up. The sun was getting hot and I was starting to sweat. Mick took off his t-shirt and stuffed it down inside his jeans. His back was long and arched and deep brown from the heat of summer. I wished my skin was like that. I could see the bones of his spine, almost like he was a lizard.

He nodded toward the side of the track.

'There,' he said.

I couldn't see anything.

'Where?'

'There,' he said, and pointed this time.

The scrub was pretty thick, all prickly bushes and old gum trees that were twisted and dry. Most of them were too close together, so the trunks were skinny and sick looking.

We left our bikes and walked through the scrub toward an old fence. It was one of those really old ones with grey posts that are almost falling over. The barbed wire was rusty and loose.

When we got close I could see. Tippy was lying down almost like he was asleep, except his mouth was open and his tongue was hanging out. There were flies on him. Mostly where his fur was matted, where the bullet went into his side, but in his mouth too.

Mick hocked something in his throat and spat it out.

I wondered why someone had shot Tippy, but I couldn't really talk. My eyes started to burn and I swallowed hard, trying to stop the feeling inside my throat that always comes before I cry. I didn't want to be a sook.

'Who did it?' I said.

Mick shrugged. 'Dunno. Some prick.'

Even if some prick had shot him, I knew it was my fault. If I'd been more careful, Tippy wouldn't have got away. If I'd been more careful, he wouldn't have got shot.

We stood there for a bit, not saying anything. I could hear the heat almost as much as I could feel it. The hum of blowflies, the crackling of bark, and that slow, lazy call the magpies make when it gets hot. Like they're bored with the world and everything in it.

Mick passed me the shovel.

'C'mon,' he said. 'Better get started.'

•

Mick didn't ride as quick on the way back. And he let me ride a bit closer. Not right next to him, though. Just a few metres behind.

About halfway home, when we got past the rifle range, he stopped and turned to face me. He looked me in the eyes, which he almost never does.

'You all right?' he said.

'Yep.'

I think it's the only time he's ever asked me anything like that, so I remember it really clear. It was nice he asked, but it made me sad too. I'm not sure why. Then he said I could go to the mechanics with him to get the Pacer, as long as I kept quiet.

•

When I think about it now, I wish I hadn't seen Tippy like that. Because some things can't be unseen. But more than that, some things can't be undone. That's what Mick says.

And even though he's wrong about some things, most things really, he's probably right about that.

PART ONE

ONE

February is the hottest month of the year, so I reckon it's a pretty cruel time to send kids back to school. I like summer, mostly. I just don't like school that much.

There's hardly any shade at our school, just one big peppercorn tree that makes your hands sticky if you touch the leaves. Most of the yard is boiling hot asphalt. On the really hot days, the asphalt goes soft under your feet.

In summer, us boys play cricket out on the oval, and the girls do their own thing. Me and Danny aren't that good at cricket, not like the sporty kids, but we still join in when they need the numbers. We hardly ever get to bat or bowl, though. We usually just field, and mostly at fine leg or third man. It's pretty boring.

In winter the sporty kids play footy, which I like even less than cricket. At least in cricket, when you're fielding, you can keep quiet and stay out of the way. You can look like you're part of something even when you're not.

One of the main things I don't like about school in summer is the swimming carnival. I hate the swimming training before it too, but we don't do that every year.

The athletics carnival is heaps better, but that's in winter. Tunnel ball is probably my favourite, or long jump. One of those two.

The swimming carnival happens at the Mittigunda Leisure Complex. Leisure Complex is just a fancy name for a pool, two squash courts and an indoor cricket pitch.

The pool is especially crap. Its walls are cracked and it stinks like chemicals. They've been talking about building a new pool for years. There's a fundraising sign out the front, with a big thermometer showing how much money they've raised. They need a hundred thousand dollars and they've only got about twenty thousand, so I don't think it'll ever happen.

I don't mind being in the water, but I can't swim. Not properly. That's the main problem. And pretty much everyone else at school can, even some of the grade ones and preps. It's embarrassing.

Charlie told Mum that he's gonna teach me. Charlie is sort of like Mum's boyfriend, but he doesn't live with us. For a few weeks he stayed at our place, but then he moved out again. His place is a cabin out at the caravan park. It looks like a tin shed, but with a little timber deck out front.

Charlie's tall and skinny, with black hair slicked over to one side. He has sideburns down his cheeks, and green tattoos on his forearms. He told me and Sam once that he used to be in the army in Vietnam, and that's why he got the tattoos.

There's no pictures of girls or animals on his arms, just words and numbers. It's hard to read them properly because he has his sleeves rolled down most of the time. The biggest tattoo says '5RAR'. I'm not sure what it means. He said he got the tattoos after the war, because you weren't allowed to have them while you were serving.

'Only in the navy,' he said. 'And I was never up for that.'

Charlie doesn't say much, but he's all right to me. He's mostly nice to Sam too, which I think is the main reason Mum likes him. I've heard her saying it on the phone to Aunty Pam.

But she doesn't tell Aunty Pam everything.

She doesn't tell her about the times Charlie gets angry, or about the time he pushed her.

When Charlie pushed Mum, me and Sam saw the whole thing. Sam got scared and ran out of the house and down the street, but I caught up with him pretty quick. I don't know where he was headed, but he was really upset.

Charlie's promised Mum that won't ever happen again, that he won't push her, but she still made him move back to his cabin at the caravan park.

I think Mum doesn't tell Aunty Pam about any of that because she doesn't want her to worry.

Most times Charlie talks to Sam like he's normal, which is good. He's especially nice to Sam in front of Mum, but different when she's not around. Even so, he's better than some people. Some people talk to Sam like he's a baby, which annoys me a bit. Other people just ignore him, or look away, which is even worse.

Mum thinks it'll be good if Charlie teaches me how to swim, but I'm worried it'll be embarrassing. Not as embarrassing as the swimming carnival, but almost. I can't really imagine Charlie going to the pool. I can't really imagine him swimming either. Mostly he's off shearing somewhere, or working on his car, or drinking cans of Carlton Light.

Charlie's car is a maroon Kingswood, and it's nice when it's going. But it has a lot of problems. Not as many as his old ute, but almost. It's nowhere near as nice as Mick's Pacer, but I'd never say that to Charlie.

•

Charlie reckons we'll go on Sunday, after he gets back from helping some farmer with a fencing job. We're not going to the pool, though. And Mum says she can't come.

'I have to go see Nan,' she says.

We all used to go see Nan on Sundays at the nursing home before she died. Mick used to come too, before he went to jail.

I would have much preferred to go with Mum to see Nan at the cemetery than go for a swim, but I couldn't say so.

It was last year when she died, but it still seems really recent. I liked Nan a lot. She was skinny as a stick and lived at the nursing home for almost as long as I can remember. She was married once, but I never knew my pop because he was dead before I was born.

Like I said, me and Mum and Sam used to go see Nan every Sunday. Mick would come too, but not as often. We'd always get dressed up nicer when we went. I had to wear my good shoes, which were way too tight and incredibly uncomfortable.

The nursing home was called The Oakview, but I'm not sure why. The carpet was dark blue and everything smelled a bit like perfume, but with something else underneath. Some of the people who worked there wore white gumboots.

Nan's memory wasn't very good, and sometimes she'd tell the same stories over and over. Sometimes she'd start the same story right after she'd just finished it, so you'd have to listen all over again and pretend it was new. It was okay, once you got used to it.

Mum was always cross when we were there. She'd always complain to the nursing home people about something, but mostly about the food. The food did look pretty terrible, to be honest. It was nearly always mashed potato, pumpkin, or savs with tomato sauce.

'You wouldn't serve it to a dog,' she said.

It made me embarrassed when she said things like that, and I could tell the nursing home people didn't like it. I don't think the food was their fault.

One time, after we left, I asked Mum why she got so cross.

'I don't like how they look after her,' she said. 'She deserves better.'

Sometimes, I wonder why Mum and Aunty Pam didn't take Nan out of there. If they took her home, she would've been looked after better, and we would have seen her more often. And she might have lived for longer.

But I've never said anything about it. And after she died, it was too late.

•

Me and Sam sit in the back of the Kingswood, which is where we normally sit. Me on the right side, him on the left. Sam doesn't like it if I sit on the left. But without Mum in the car, it feels different. She usually does most of the talking.

Charlie turns the corner into Macpherson Street. Because I'm the oldest, I feel like I should say something.

'How many cars have you had?'

Charlie eyes me in the rear-view mirror.

'A few.'

He reaches into the console beside him, takes out a pack of smokes. Charlie only smokes Craven A Filters. I know the brand because he gives me money sometimes to buy them from the milk bar. They cost one dollar seventy, but he gives me two dollars and lets me keep the change. I usually spend it on mixed lollies for me and Sam.

He dangles the cigarette between his lips but doesn't light it.

'Is this the nicest car you've had?'

He nods. 'She's all right. When she's running.'

I'm not sure what to say after that. The quiet in the car gets louder, and I wonder if Charlie can hear it too.

After a bit he says, 'How's your mum been?'

'Good,' I say.

He eyes me again in the rear-view.

'She had any fellas over?'

It's not the first time Charlie has asked me, so I know what to say.

'Nah.'

'You sure?'

'Yep.'

Once we turn onto the highway, he pushes the lighter button in and waits till it pops back out. He lights his smoke and winds down the window. The warm air rushes inside, the car speeds up, and everything feels more relaxed after that.

When we're out of town, he puts on the radio. It's country and western, and the static is pretty bad. Someone is singing about being lonesome, which is what they're nearly always singing about. Charlie tries to tune the radio better, but it doesn't work. He starts tapping the steering wheel anyway, like he knows the song. I don't like country and western that much, but I'm happy we don't have to talk. I think he is too.

Soon, we're out in the middle of the farms where the cows and sheep live. The paddocks look all yellow and dry. Eventually, Charlie turns off the highway and drives up a dirt road. It's corrugated and dusty. He makes me wind up my window, but the dust still gets inside from somewhere. The radio is out of range, so he switches it off. After a bit, he slows the car down and pulls over to the side of the road.

'Here we are,' he says.

I look out and there's nothing but empty paddocks. We get out of the car and it feels hotter than it was in town. The air smells like dry grass and dust, and flies come in from every-where. On the other side of the road, there's a paddock with a couple of tall gum trees a little way from the fence. I can see there's a dam underneath the trees. It looks muddy and brown and pretty crap. My heart sinks a bit.

Charlie shields his eyes from the sun, looks all around. There's no houses or sheds or anything for miles, just endless paddocks of dry grass and fences. He goes to the back of the car and pops the boot. He takes out a long coil of rope, then slings it over his shoulder.

'This is Bluey's farm,' he says.

'Who's Bluey?'

'An old mate.'

We follow Charlie to the fence. He spreads the wires apart and lets me and Sam climb through. Sam goes first. The grass is long and yellow, almost up to my waist. Sam runs off ahead.

'Wait,' I say. 'There might be snakes.'

He stops and looks at me. I smile like I didn't really mean it. He waits till we catch up, takes hold of my hand.

As we walk toward the dam, Sam starts humming. Mum calls it singing, and she reckons he might be famous one day. I think she's just being nice.

When we get to the dam, Charlie tells me to take off my t-shirt. I do what he says. Sam crouches down near the dam's edge and starts drawing in the mud with a stick.

'Be careful, mate,' Charlie says. 'Don't get your shoes wet.'

Sam can't swim either, but no one has ever tried to teach him. Maybe they have at the Special School, but I doubt it.

Charlie unwinds the coil of rope, loops it under my arms, and ties it around my chest. It's rough on my skin and smells like oil. His hands work quick, like he's used the rope heaps of times before. Sam starts humming again.

'What's the rope for?' I say.

'Just a back-up. In case you get into trouble.'

Charlie takes the loose end, then sits down on the bank next to Sam. He reaches into his top pocket and takes out his smokes.

He lights one with a match, and Sam watches him closely. Sam loves matches, so Mum always keeps them hidden at home.

I look into the water and wonder how deep it is. I wonder if there's fish and yabbies in there, and if the yabbies might bite me. I don't want to go in, but I know I don't have much choice. Charlie has gone to the trouble to bring us out here, and I don't want him to get cross.

The mud is thick and sticky, and it squelches up between my toes. The water is unbelievably cold.

'You'll be right,' Charlie says. 'And I've got the rope, remember? In case you get into strife.'

Sam starts clapping.

I go further out, up to my knees, with my feet sinking deeper into the mud, up to my ankles. Once I'm up to my waist, I can feel the bank slipping sharply into deeper water.

Charlie stands up and walks around the bank to the other side of the dam, still holding the end of the rope. Sam follows. When he gets to the other side, Charlie flicks his smoke in the water. The butt floats like a dead insect, and I cross my arms to try to keep warm.

'Go on then,' he says. 'Swim toward me.'

I start shivering.

'I can't.'

'Just have a crack. It's a confidence thing.'

Maybe he's right. I just need to try and eventually it'll happen. I could start swimming like the other kids, like people in the Olympics.

I take a deep breath and dive forward into the water. The cold makes the air stop in my chest. I pull at the water, but quickly start sinking. I open my mouth for air, but only water rushes in. It's dark and I'm sinking deeper and deeper. There's nothing under my feet. I feel the rope slide up under my armpits, and I grab hold and try to pull myself up. My head comes out of the water for a second, and I hear Charlie yelling, but the rope slides from my hands and I sink back down. Everything is dark and cold and endless.

For the first time ever, I'm scared I might die.

The rope pulls hard under my arms, and I reach and grab hold again. I can feel Charlie pulling. It feels like forever, but my shoulder finally hits the muddy bank on the other side. I crawl up out of the water on my hands and knees. I cough my guts out until I spew.

Charlie comes in close, puts a hand on my shoulder.

'You all right?'

I cough and spew again. It's all water and dirt and it tastes disgusting.

'Sorry, mate,' he says.

Charlie goes to the car to get a towel. I start feeling a bit better, but my throat is sore from the spew. When he comes back I dry myself off. Charlie lights another smoke. He shakes his head.

'Jesus, Jimmy. You sink like a stone.' He takes a deep drag. 'It's like your bones are made of lead.'

Sam starts humming again.

'I always sink,' I say. 'I don't know how people do it.'

Charlie finishes his smoke, then flicks the butt into the dam.

'You should be going like this.'

He shows me what looks like freestyle, but not exactly.

'Keep your head up, do that over and over, and you'll be right.'

I finish drying myself off and put my t-shirt back on. It's warm from the sun.

'You wanna have another crack?' he says.

'Nah.'

'You sure?'

'Yep.'

'Head home then?'

'Yep.'

Charlie starts winding the rope back up into a coil. He does it over his forearm and shoulder, and it looks like something he's done a million times before. I wonder if he learned it in the army.

'I never liked swimming that much myself,' he says. 'Another reason I stayed away from the navy.'

Sam is still humming, and Charlie gives him a look.

'Jesus, Sam, will you shut the fuck up?'

Sam looks at him and stops humming. It's the sort of thing Charlie would never say in front of Mum.

Sam picks up a new stick, then pokes it into the mud. Charlie takes my towel and slings it over his shoulder with the rope.

'Thanks, Charlie,' I say.

I take Sam's hand in mine to walk back to the car. I give it a squeeze.

'We'll have another go next week,' Charlie says. 'If we keep at it, you'll come good.'

•

At school on Monday, I tell Danny.

'You going again?' he says.

I shake my head. 'Not if I can help it.'

Danny reckons I should do proper swimming lessons, but I know Mum could never afford it.

'I'll teach you then,' he says.

Danny is a pretty good swimmer. His family even go on holidays to the beach sometimes, but they mostly go to Lake Redfin. It isn't like they're super rich or anything.

'Where?' I say.

'Where do you reckon? The pool.'

'Nah. It's too embarrassing.'

'At a dam then. What about that place we went last year? The one with all the yabbies.'

'Nah.'

Danny frowns.

'What about Chadwick's?' he says.

'Chadwick's?'

'Yeah.'

Chadwick's name is Luke, but everyone calls him Chadwick. He's in our year, but in the other class. His family moved to Mittigunda from Sydney last year. He has black curly hair, and everyone says he's really smart. Maybe even the smartest kid in the school. He's kind of weird, because he acts a bit up himself even though he's a nerd.

'He's got a pool,' Danny says.

Chadwick does have a pool, a proper one. It's in-ground. Me and Danny saw it when we were riding our bikes up Wilson Street one time. We stopped and looked over his back fence, using our bikes for ladders. It wasn't as big as the public pool, but the water looked really clean and blue.

Chadwick's dad is a lawyer, so Chadwick always has the newest runners and the best cricket gear and all the latest stuff. He's even got a Twin Scoop Gray Nicolls, which me and Danny know costs two hundred and ninety-nine dollars, because we saw it at Top Sports. And he isn't even that good at cricket.

He's still a nerd, though. Some kids are like that, no matter what stuff they've got.

'Will I ask him then?' Danny says.

I shrug.

The rumour is that Chadwick's parents are going to send him to some really posh boarding school in Sydney, once he finishes primary. Mainly because he's so good at maths and stuff, but also because his dad went there.

That's really everything I know about him.

TWO

Sam doesn't go to my primary school in Mittigunda. It's probably just as well.

He goes to the Special School. That's what it's called. It's also called 'Emerald River' by some people, mostly grown-ups, because it's right near the Emerald River. That river is nearly always dried up, though. It's no good for fishing or yabbying or anything really. You can get some taddies there for bait, but that's about it. And it stinks a bit, like sewage.

Some kids give me and Sam a hard time because we hold hands. They call us homos, which is completely stupid. They don't do it when Mick is around. Most kids are pretty scared of Mick.

Sam is two years younger than me, but I don't know what grade he's in at the Special School. I don't even know if they have grades like a normal school. They don't have reports or parent–teacher interviews, as far as I know. I think they just do activities all day. Like making coloured paper chains with Clag. Sam's always bringing them home, and Mum is always making a big deal of it.

Mum says Sam's got some type of syndrome, but it's pretty severe. He doesn't talk much, only a few words. But you can understand him, once you get to know him. I can tell when he's upset, and when he's happy. I can tell mostly by the look in his eyes.

He's especially happy when he's got his Rubik's Cube. He takes it pretty much everywhere. Mum bought it for him for Christmas. He used to love cards too, playing cards, but he's sick of those now. He'd arrange them, rearrange them, stack them up. He has about five decks, because that's what Mum got him for birthdays and Christmas, up until he got the Rubik's Cube.

The bus to the Special School picks Sam up most days. He doesn't get the normal bus, because they have their own. Sam's bus stops right outside our house, and there are usually a few of the others on it. Like Neville, who's about Mick's age. He's really tall and wiry and has a face like a bird. He has an earring.

Mick's got one too, a sleeper, and I'd like to get one when I'm older. I know Mum will never let me do it now, so I don't ask.

Veronica is nearly always on the bus too. She smiles at me. She smiles at everything, though. Danny says she's got Down's syndrome, but only a bit. He also says she wants to marry me, which he thinks is hilarious.

When Mum's doing an afternoon shift she tells Don, the bus driver, to drop Sam at my school. I have to wait for him at the bus stop then walk home from there. Danny usually waits with me, because he lives in Arnold Street, which is the next street over from our place.

Danny's a real smartarse. This year we're in grade five and in the same class. Grade four was different. The teacher reckoned Danny was 'disruptive' when we were together, so they put him in the other class. We got to see each other at recess and lunch, but it wasn't the same.

I try to get good marks at school. When I get an okay report, it makes Mum happy. But it gets harder every year. Mick used to help me with some of it, before he went to jail. I'm terrible at maths, and he was better at it.

Danny pokes me in the ribs when the bus turns the corner.

'What?' I say.

'Just thinking.'

'Yeah?'

'Yeah.'

'About what?'

'About how you should go to the Special School too. Family discount.'

'Get stuffed.'

Sam's bus is noisy as ever, the engine whining and grinding up the road. It's more like a minibus, but it still makes heaps of noise. It shudders to a stop against the gutter, with hissing brakes and fumes. It's a crap bus. Way worse than the one for our school.

The hydraulic door thing creaks open. Don looks out and smiles. His face is sweaty.

'Sorry I'm late, boys.'

He pulls the handbrake on, unbuckles his seatbelt, then walks up the back of the bus to get Sam. He leaves the engine running. Don takes Sam by the hand, then leads him down to the front.

That's the thing with Sam. Someone nearly always has to be holding his hand for him to walk anywhere. Not because he can't walk on his own, but because he likes having his hand held.

Don climbs down the steps and gives me a wink.

'How's it going, Jimmy?'

'Good.'

Don has white hair and he's really skinny. He looks about eighty, but I'm not sure exactly how old he is. It's hard to tell with people who are really old. He used to drive the normal bus, but he got moved to the special bus about a year ago after he nearly killed everyone.

We were on the way home from school when it happened, in the middle of summer. Don was driving us over the train crossing at Manningham Street and the bus stalled. He couldn't get it going again. Normally it wouldn't have mattered, except there was a freight train coming.

The back end of the bus was on the tracks, so everyone freaked out and ran to the front. I could tell Don was panicking because he was jumping around in his seat like his pants were on fire. The train was getting closer and its horn was so loud and you could hear the wheels screeching on the tracks. It was scary as.

Don got the bus going just in time and it jolted forward. He stalled it again, but everyone was so relieved to be off the tracks. We all clapped and cheered like he was a hero.

Some of the parents found out after, though, and they complained to the school. Mum told me about it. By the next week, he didn't drive our bus anymore.

The bus company replaced him with someone much younger. His name is Bernard and he wears dark sunglasses that go all the way around to the sides. He isn't as friendly as Don. He's never stalled the bus, though. Not even once.

Don eyes me. 'How's your mum?'

'All right.'

Mum has always liked Don, and she reckons what happened was the bus company's fault. She said the buses were too old, and the other parents were wrong to blame Don for it. She said they should have boom gates at the crossing too, and they were just looking for a scapegoat. That's what she said.

Don scratches his chin. 'Haven't seen her in a while.'

I shrug.

'Busy with work then?'

'Yep,' I say. 'I spose.'

'Well, that's good.' He roughs Sam's hair. 'See you tomorrow, Sam. These two will look after you, won't you, boys?'

'Yep,' I say.

I take Sam's hand. It's sticky.

Danny pats Sam on the shoulder. 'How was school?'

'Okay.'

He doesn't look at Danny when he says it, keeps his eyes down. 'Mum?' he says.

I squeeze his hand. 'Yep, we're gonna see Mum. But first we'll go to the milk bar. You wanna go to the milk bar?'

'Okay.'

'Okay' is probably Sam's favourite word. He uses it nearly all the time. Sometimes he says it when it doesn't make much sense. Times when things aren't okay.

•

The milk bar isn't on the way home. It's down the other end of Richardson Street, near the railway station. Danny wanted to walk on the railway line to get there.

The sun always feels hotter down on the railway line. The tracks are at the bottom of a cutting, so not much wind gets in. There isn't a lot of room, so if a train comes, you have to run and press your body against the sides. The earth is all scratchy on your skin, and the train driver always goes crazy with his horn. It's deafening, and it makes our ears ring for ages.

Danny reckons it's quicker to walk the railway line to get to the milk bar, but we've never timed it to check if he's right.

The milk bar is probably my favourite shop in town. It's better than Greasy Pete's, which is Danny's favourite. A new family has taken over running the milk bar. The old owner, Mrs Greenwood, left town. I don't know where she went. Mum said she left almost everything she owned behind. She left after her son died.

His name was Travis Greenwood. He was Mick's best mate.

Travis Greenwood had a black moustache and he walked with a limp. He almost always wore the same red flannelette shirt, but Danny reckoned he probably had more than one. Danny said he had a limp because one leg was shorter than the other, but I don't know if that's true. Danny also reckoned he was murdered, but I know he made that up because he couldn't remember who told him.

When I asked Mum how Travis Greenwood died, she didn't really answer at first. She was pretty upset. Then she said it was a car crash.

If I'm honest, I didn't like Travis Greenwood much. It was mainly because he used his fingers to bag the mixed lollies instead of the tongs. The tongs were right there, and Mrs Greenwood always used them. I never said anything, though, because he was best mates with Mick. He was mates with Mick even though Mick was a few years younger than him. He was always really serious too, and he hardly ever smiled. I was a bit scared of him.

Even though I didn't like him much, I'm sorry he died. Sorry for Mrs Greenwood. Sorry for Mum, too, because I think she liked him. But mainly sorry for Mick. Mick was in jail when it happened, which would've made it worse.

Mum had to tell him over the phone, and she almost cried when she did it. She was even more upset after, because I heard her crying in her room. I wasn't sure if she was crying for Mick, or for Travis Greenwood. Maybe both.

The new family are really nice, though. They're Chinese. The lady is tiny and she can barely reach over the counter. Her name is Mrs Chen. She's shorter than me, even though she's grown up. She sometimes gives me and Sam stuff for free, or cheaper than the normal price. She never says much apart from 'Hello!', and then she laughs like it's the funniest thing ever. Her husband only speaks Chinese, so whenever a customer comes in he always calls out for her in words I don't understand.

Mrs Chen smiles a lot. More than Mrs Greenwood did. Definitely more than Travis Greenwood. And she always uses the tongs.

Danny walks the train rail like he's on a tightrope in the circus, his arms stretched out for balance.

'Got a coin?' he says.

'Yeah, but I need it.'

I figure he can use his own coins, because some of the shops won't take them after they get flattened. And they don't work in the games at Greasy Pete's, either.

We always listen out for trains when we're down in the cutting because sometimes they come quicker than you expect. There aren't as many trains as there used to be. Mostly just the freight ones, like the one that nearly killed us when the bus stalled.

The freight trains are pretty boring, but Danny likes them. They're really long and have big steel containers. Danny reckons they're filled with petrol or grain or oil, but he isn't completely sure.

The best train is the *Southern Aurora*. It goes all the way from Melbourne to Sydney, and from Sydney to Melbourne. It stops in Mittigunda because we're pretty much exactly halfway between, so some of the crew can change over. The *Southern Aurora* is first class only, so it's really fancy. It even has dining and sleeper carriages, and it only runs at night.

I don't know why it's called the *Southern Aurora*. Danny reckons it's because it comes from Melbourne, which is in the south. But that doesn't explain the aurora bit, and it actually runs both ways.

Danny has been on it once when he went to Melbourne, which is how I know it's only first class. I asked Mum if we can go on it one day, and she said, 'Maybe.' She said we might go once Mick is out of jail.

'Could make a weekend of it,' she said. 'Go to Melbourne and do some shopping. Get you boys some nice clothes.'

I really hope we'll do it one day, but there isn't much time because Danny reckons they're gonna replace the *Southern Aurora* soon. He says they're gonna replace it with the *Melbourne Express* and the *Sydney Express*. It'll just be one train, but with a different name depending on which direction it's going. I don't think it'll be all first class like the *Southern Aurora*.

Danny says they're gonna call the *Melbourne Express* 'Mex', and the *Sydney Express* 'Sex', which he thinks is pretty funny.

At the milk bar, I get a can of Fanta, and a Barney Banana for Sam. I'm short five cents, but Mrs Chen lets me have it anyway. I promise I'll pay her back, but she just shakes her head and smiles. Danny said he was gonna get a few Redskins, but he buys a bag of Wizz Fizz and a Coke instead.

We sit outside on the footpath with our legs stretched out and our backs against the wall. The bricks still feel nice and warm from the sun, even though we're in the shade. Sam bites into his Barney Banana and takes nearly half in one go.

'You're sposed to lick it,' Danny says. 'Take it slow, or you'll get brain freeze.'

Sam keeps eating.

I drink my Fanta slowly. Not because of brain freeze, but because I want to enjoy it. It's icy, sweet and really delicious.

Danny drinks his Coke super quick. When Danny drinks, he tilts his head back like he's pouring it straight down his throat, with his eyes squinting to the sun. Then he does a big 'Ahhhh' and smiles, like he's on TV or something. Like it's the best thing ever. It's kind of annoying when he does it, but pretty funny too.

He puts the empty in his backpack, takes mine too. We've been saving cans to take them to the Cash-a-Can place, but they never give us much. Danny reckons their ads on TV are false advertising, because they make out like you're gonna get rich.

He stands up, slings his bag over his shoulder.

'What do you wanna do?' he says.

'Dunno.'

'Tech School?'

'What for?'

He shrugs. 'Look for balls?'

The Tech School is pretty crap. It's just a big four-storey building with a patch of dry, weedy grass out front. It doesn't even have a proper oval or anything. It's always really windy, and last time we only found two tennis balls in the gutter near the carpark, and one was cracked.

Dumb kids go to the Tech School, Danny reckons. They go there instead of going to the high school. Mick went to the Tech School, until he got expelled. Mick's smart in some ways, but not so much at school stuff. Apart from maths.

The Tech School is where you study to be a plumber or a carpenter, that sort of thing. It's also where some kids meet for a fight after school, but I'm not sure why. Either there or at the reservation, which everyone calls the resi.

One time, Danny brought his skateboard to the Tech School, and we took turns riding it down the concrete path that runs all the way from the main door to the carpark. It was pretty cool. The second time he tried it, he fell and took heaps of skin off his shoulder. It was bleeding pretty bad, but he acted like it didn't hurt. We decided to go home after that. I saw him crying a bit on the way, even if he tried to do it quiet.

It's the only time I've ever seen Danny cry, and I felt bad for him. His shoulder must've really hurt. But I think his heart hurt too. His heart and shoulder were hurting all at once. The heart's always worse, I think.

Sam finishes his Barney Banana. I take the stick off him, because one time he chewed and swallowed some of it.

'Mum,' he says.

'I better take him home. Mum'll be back by now. She'll start to worry.'

'Mum.'

'Yeah, yeah.' I take his hand.

Danny crosses his arms. 'C'mon. We'll just go for a bit. Won't take long.'

Danny is always saying that. Nothing ever takes very long, but then you're there for hours.

'Nah. Mum'll be worried if we're late.'

That's part of the truth. I do need to go home. But it isn't just because Mum will be worried.

And even though Danny is my best friend in the world, and I can tell him almost anything, he doesn't need to know about that.

THREE

The Kaiser is made by a company called Kaiser Stuhl. It sounds German, but it says on the cask that it's made in South Australia. Sometimes she gets a different brand, but the Kaiser is definitely Mum's favourite.

When I get home from school, I have to check the Kaiser to see how heavy it is, because that's the only way to tell. When she's happy, she doesn't need the Kaiser as much. That's what I've learned. But I've also learned the sooner we get home, the better. Then I can keep an eye on her, and an eye on the Kaiser.

Things will be easier once Mick gets out of jail. She's not as bad when Mick's around. Even though he gets angry at some people, he's never angry at her. He gets angry at me sometimes, but never at Sam.

But I worry he'll get in trouble again when he gets out, and I have other feelings about it too. Things I talk to Sam about on the way home.

'You think he'll be angry?'

'Yep.'

'He's angry a lot of the time, isn't he?'

'Okay.'

'You remember?'

'Yep.'

'You think he'll be nicer to me this time?'

'Yep.'

'You're probably right.'

Talking to Sam nearly always makes me feel better. Talking to Nan used to help too.

Mick was in jail when she died, so he missed the funeral. Mum was upset because she reckoned he could've got 'special leave'. I told her it probably wasn't Mick's fault, that maybe he didn't know about special leave.

Aunty Pam came, though. She's really nice, but she doesn't live in Mittigunda. She lives in Fernvale, which is a few hours away.

She took me and Sam to the church in her car, while Mum went with Charlie in his old ute. Aunty Pam's car's a yellow Ford Escort. It's only little, but it's really clean inside and smells like pine trees.

When Aunty Pam picked us up, her and Mum didn't say very much to each other. I think they were both too sad. Aunty Pam had a black dress on, and I could see the edges of her undies showing through, like her dress was way too tight.

On the way to the church, Sam started humming. Aunty Pam told him that she really liked his voice, but he'd have to be quiet during the funeral.

I asked her why Nan died. I didn't want to ask Mum because I didn't want her to get upset again, like when she first found out Nan had died, or when Mick told her he couldn't come.

Aunty Pam looked at me, then the road, then me again. She waited till we'd stopped at a stop sign. She said it was Nan's leg that killed her. She said it was the nursing home's fault because they should have looked after her better.

'The ulcer on her leg opened up and it got infected. Then her blood got infected. That's what did it.'

I never saw the ulcer on Nan's leg, not even once, but it sounds pretty awful. Aunty Pam said Nan had the ulcer for years, because she used to be a cook. I knew she'd been a cook, but I didn't know about the ulcer.

'On her feet most of her life,' she said. 'She deserved better than how things ended up.'

It was a bit like what Mum had said.

The funeral was really sad. The priest was skinny as a skeleton, and talked about Heaven and God and Jesus, but hardly said anything about Nan.

Aunty Pam said it was my job to look after Sam in the church, so I didn't get to think about Nan as much as I wanted to. Sam mostly stayed quiet. I think it was because he was sad too. I know he really liked Nan.

Charlie carried the coffin with three of the funeral home people, who tried their best to look upset, even if they didn't really know Nan. I reckon they didn't ask me because I'm too short.

On the way to the cemetery, Aunty Pam said Charlie did a good thing to help carry the coffin.

'It shows respect. That's important,' she said. 'You'll realise that more when you're older. He shows more respect than your dad ever did.'

I don't know much about my dad. He was dead before I was born. Sam had a different dad, but Mick has the same one as me.

Mick remembers our dad, but I'm not allowed to ask anything about him. It's one of Mick's rules. He has a few of those.

When I think about it, some things are easier when Mick's inside. But I'd never say that out loud. Anyway, he might be different when he gets out. Maybe he's learned some lessons, because he's in a different jail. Maybe he'll be nicer this time.

FOUR

It's the next Saturday when me and Danny are meant to go to Chadwick's, but I don't really want to.

'It isn't even gonna be hot,' I say.

Danny organised it with Chadwick earlier in the week, before we knew what the weather was gonna be like.

'It's already sorted,' he says. 'Can't back out now.'

Danny isn't the most popular kid, but Chadwick is a level down from him. I'm a level down from Danny too, even though we're friends. At the top is David Knight, who's good at everything, but especially sport.

Chadwick hangs around with Bradley Whitehead and Stephen Murphy. Both those kids are a bit weird, which makes

Chadwick a bit weird too, even if he has all that great stuff. So when Danny asked him if we could go over and use his pool, Chadwick was pretty keen. I think it was like his big chance to go up a level.

Mum said I have to take Sam with me. I don't mind, but I didn't tell Chadwick or Danny that I was bringing him along.

Me and Sam have to walk to Chadwick's house, which takes ages. Sam can't ride a bike, which is crap because it means I have to walk everywhere when I take him places. And apart from the trip to the dam, Charlie hardly ever takes us anywhere in his car. Especially if Mum isn't going. It's not on purpose, I don't think, but because his car nearly always has problems.

Danny is waiting out front when we get there, his bike leaning against the fence.

'What took you so long?' he says.

I give him a look. 'What do you think?'

Sam's brought his Rubik's Cube with him, and he starts working on it again. He has the blue side mostly done.

It's the first time I've looked properly at Chadwick's house from the front. It's yellow brick and double storey, but you can only see the top half from the street because there's a big wooden fence running the full width. There's a driveway with a big steel gate, and a smaller wooden gate beside it. Both are closed.

The house goes back really deep, and there's a couple of palm trees down the side, like it's in *Miami Vice* or something.

There aren't any mansions in Mittigunda but Chadwick's house is probably the nearest thing to one.

Danny smiles, like he knows what I'm thinking.

'Nice, isn't it?'

I shrug.

'It's gonna be great to check it out. He'll have some good stuff. It'll be like the mothership of good stuff.'

It's weird Chadwick's house is the biggest in Mittigunda, because he doesn't have any brothers or sisters. It's just him and his mum and dad. I haven't seen his dad the lawyer before, but I've seen his mum outside the school a couple of times. She wears big round sunglasses and has red hair. She looks a bit posh.

I push the wooden gate, but it's locked.

'How do we get in?'

Danny grins. 'I wondered the same thing. Check this out.'

Beside the gate, built into the fence, is a small metallic box. It has a speaker with a red button in the middle.

'What is it?' I say.

'An intercom. Flash as.'

He puts his mouth near the speaker, then presses the button.

'Hello?' he says.

After a few seconds, someone answers. It might have been Mrs Chadwick, but I can't really be sure. It's mostly static.

The gate clicks open.

Danny shakes his head, eyes wide.

'How cool is that?'

•

As it turns out, I'm right. The covers are on the pool and Chadwick says it isn't hot enough to go swimming. Nowhere near.

But Danny is right as well. Chadwick has heaps of great stuff. He has the best stuff I've ever seen.

We play in the rumpus room pretty much all day. I'd never been in a rumpus room before, and I didn't really know what one was. It's like a lounge room, with a couple of armchairs and a coffee table, plus a big TV. But it has heaps of games and stuff too. That's probably the main difference from a lounge room.

Chadwick has a racing car set in one corner, which looks like it's set up permanent. We play that for ages, but I'm pretty crap at it. The cars keep coming off at the bends. He has Test Match set up in another corner, but we don't get time to play it. It has the green felt field glued to a big wooden board, so it doesn't curl up when you're playing. That's always the problem with Test Match when we play at Danny's, even if his mum irons it.

Mrs Chadwick keeps Sam with her, which is nice, even if I thought it was a bit weird at first.

'Sam can watch television with me in the lounge room,' she said.

She says 'television' instead of 'TV' or 'telly', like she's in the royal family.

I see them when I go to the toilet. Sam looks pretty happy, even if he isn't watching the telly. Neither of them are. He's staring at his Rubik's Cube, like he's thinking about his next move, and Mrs Chadwick is reading a book called *The Thorn Birds*. There's no birds on the cover, though, just people standing around.

I've never seen my mum read a book, but she reads the newspaper and magazines sometimes. Charlie reads the form guide, because it's about horses and greyhound racing. Those are the only things I see them read. Mick has two books in his room. They're written by Stephen King, and they're really thick. One's called *Salem's Lot* and the other's called *The Stand*. I think he must've borrowed them from Travis Greenwood, because Greenwood's name is written on the first page of each of them. I've never seen Mick read them, though.

Even though Chadwick has all that great stuff, the best bit is at lunchtime. Mrs Chadwick cooks us a proper lunch, not just Vegemite or peanut butter sandwiches like we have at home. She makes us hamburgers, which are delicious. And she squeezes real orange juice, which is sweet and sour all at once.

Chadwick doesn't talk much, apart from explaining the stuff he has in the rumpus room. He's pretty good on the racing car set, and at Meccano. I've never seen so much Meccano. He says some of it is from when his dad was a kid, and some of it his dad bought him for his birthdays. We spend most of the afternoon playing with it, once we decide there isn't enough time for Test Match. Danny keeps looking at me with these eyes that say, *Can you believe how good this is?*

At about five o'clock, Mrs Chadwick comes in.

'Better drive you boys home,' she says.

'It's okay,' I say. 'Me and Sam can walk.'

'Don't be silly. I'm happy to drive you.'

I notice Sam has different pants on than when we got there, brown corduroy, instead of his black tracky dacks.

Mrs Chadwick sees me looking. She comes up close and whispers in my ear. She smells like lemons.

'Just a little accident,' she says. 'Nothing to worry about.'

'Okay,' I say.

Sam has accidents sometimes, but not as much as he used to.

'Tell your mum that Luke will give you the pants back at school, once I've washed them.'

I don't think Mum will care that much, but I tell Mrs Chadwick that I'll let her know anyway.

•

Mrs Chadwick's car is a Volvo station wagon, and it's boxy and orange, but kind of cheery looking. She offers to drive Danny home too, but his bike won't fit in the back.

Danny says thanks to Mrs Chadwick, and to Chadwick too, looking like he might've had the best day of his life. He even shakes Chadwick's hand, which I've never seen him do with anyone.

Me and Sam sit in the back seat, with me on the right side

and him on the left. Chadwick sits in the front beside his mum.
She looks at me in the rear-view mirror.

'What street are you boys in?'

'The Avenue,' I say. The words come out soft.

'Sorry?'

'The Avenue. Celestial Avenue.'

She smiles and starts the car.

I figure she doesn't know about the Avenue because I have
to give her directions. I thought everyone knew, but maybe she
doesn't because they're still pretty new in town. Even though its
real name is Celestial Avenue, everyone calls it the Avenue for short.

I don't really want her or Chadwick to see our house, so when
we get to the corner of the Avenue, I ask her to stop.

'You can drop us off here,' I say.

'You sure?'

'Yep.' I unbuckle my seatbelt, then Sam's. 'Thanks heaps,
Mrs Chadwick.'

'My pleasure, Jimmy. It's been lovely to have you and Sam.'
She keeps the engine running. 'Say hello to your mum for
me, okay?'

'Yep.'

She didn't know where the Avenue is, so she probably doesn't
know my mum either. I think she's just being polite. I definitely
don't reckon she knows about Mick being in jail. Most people
in Mittigunda know about the Avenue, and about Mick.

I wave to Chadwick, then take Sam's hand in mine. We walk slowly up the street toward our place. I walk as slowly as I can, and listen to the Volvo engine. I hope she'll take off before we get to our place, but she stays there for ages. I wonder if she wants to see which is our house. I wonder if she wants to see us go in. I feel my face going hot.

She calls out to me. I turn back, and she's leaning out the window.

'Don't forget what I told you,' she says. She taps the side of her nose, like it's a secret. 'Make sure you tell your mum.'

'I will. Thanks, Mrs Chadwick.'

She smiles.

'Come over again soon, okay?'

'Yep,' I say. 'We will. Definitely.'

•

It was strange how Mrs Chadwick didn't seem to know where we live. Because sometimes, no matter where we go or what we do, it feels like the whole world knows we live on the Avenue.

The Avenue is all commission houses, which means the government owns them so the rent's cheap. Mick explained it to me once.

All the houses look pretty much the same, but in different colours. Our one's lime green. Danny reckons it looks like snot, which is probably true, but I still told him off for saying it.

They're all different colours, but they all have the same cement sheets for walls, and the same aluminium windows facing out to the street. Some are bigger, like the McKenzies', and some face in a slightly different direction on their blocks, like Frank Jenkins' place. Some of the gardens are looked after nice, like Mrs Simpson's. Her front lawn is like something from a show on TV, and she's always out there trimming the grass or watering, or telling off the kids in the street for something.

Our place is probably somewhere in the middle. Not the best, but not the worst either.

We've got a bigger front yard than most because the house is further back on the block. It's really handy for Mick's Pacer because he can park it in behind the fence where no one can touch it. No one is allowed to drive Mick's car, not even Mum. He even put a cover over it before he went to jail this time. That's how much he loves it. He washed it beforehand too, even though it was already clean.

The Pacer is such a great car, and it has a really loud engine. Mick told me once that it's a 'Hemi', but I never knew what that meant. It takes up a lot of the front yard, which annoys Mum sometimes, but she puts up with it.

The front yard was good for Tippy too, before he got killed. He used to run around like a mental case when you threw the ball for him. He had a lot of energy. Maybe too much.

Two of the commission houses aren't commission houses anymore. The people who live in them bought them from the government. They're right at the end of the Avenue, so they face York Street. Their blocks are bigger than the rest, which is probably why they bought them.

One of the kids who lives there is in my year. His name is Ben Harvill, and he never talks to me much. He's one of the sporty kids, but he's not the same level as David Knight. He's pretty popular, even if he lives on the Avenue. His parents own a rubbish business, which picks up all the rubbish from the shops and takes it out to the tip in a blue truck. It has *Harvill's Waste Management* written on the side in big white letters, like it's something really fancy.

They paid fifteen thousand dollars for that place. That's what Mick told me. Fifteen thousand dollars is a lot of money. Not as much as the cash jackpot on *Sale of the Century*, or winning TattsLotto, but still a lot.

Ben Harvill never says he lives on the Avenue. He says he lives on York Street. It annoys me a bit, but I don't say anything.

•

Mum's in the lounge room watching telly when we get home. An Elvis Presley movie is on, but I can tell she isn't really watching it. She has a glass of the Kaiser in her hand.

'You boys are back late,' she says. 'Did you have a good time?'

'Yep,' I say.

She smiles at Sam, takes a sip. She doesn't notice his pants, and I don't say anything. We both sit on the couch beside her. She puts her arm around Sam. We watch the movie for a bit. It's one where he's a racing car driver. I've seen it before.

When the ads come on, I say, 'Will we ever own our own house?'

Mum frowns. 'What's brought that on?'

'Just wondering.'

She shrugs. 'Maybe one day, if we strike it lucky. If we get the money together.'

I don't think we'll ever get enough money from Mum's job, but I don't say so. She works at a factory called StormShield where they make clothes out of wool and cotton. Undies and socks, mostly, but jackets too. Mum's job isn't to make them, though. She just puts them into boxes.

She takes another sip of the Kaiser. 'But we wouldn't be buying anything like this place. We'll get something bigger and better.'

I'm not sure how that could ever happen, but it's nice she said it.

FIVE

Me and Danny are sposed to meet out the back of Margaret's Hill at nine o'clock, the same time school starts, but I'm running late.

The back wheel of my BMX is buckled, so it takes extra long. Plus, I've got Mick's slug gun in his old cricket bag, and it's rubbing on my back like crazy.

Because of the buckled wheel and because of the gun, I have to go the long way around Margaret's, instead of just straight up and over. All of this means Danny will be there before me, and I know he'll be annoyed.

But when I finally get to our usual meeting spot, he isn't there. I wait for a bit, but he still doesn't come. It's weird because Danny is nearly always on time.

I wonder if maybe he got caught wagging. It's never happened before, but maybe his parents saw him. Or someone from the school. Or the police.

I decide to ride a bit further up the road, just in case he's gone for a piss or something. And that's when I see him in one of the paddocks. There's a dam there, and he's skimming stones. But it isn't just him, he's there with Chadwick.

He hadn't said anything about inviting him along.

Danny spots me and starts walking over right away. Chadwick chucks a few more stones into the dam, then follows. I can see their bikes leaning up against the same tree, like they'd come together.

Chadwick's bike is a ripper. A red Mongoose. Unbelievable. Must've cost a fortune.

Danny climbs carefully through a gap in the barbed wire fence. He reads my look.

'Didn't think you'd mind,' he says.

I shrug, get off my bike.

'It's okay. You could've told me, though.'

To be honest, I'm a bit annoyed Danny invited him. Not so much because he hadn't told me, but because rabbiting is our thing. It's only ever me and Danny. It's one thing to go to Chadwick's house, so we can use his pool and play with his stuff, but this feels different.

Chadwick climbs through the fence. Even though he's taller than Danny, he does it easy.

'Nice bike,' I say.

'Thanks.'

I see him look at mine, but he doesn't say anything.

'Where should we go?' Danny says.

He slings his bag over his shoulder. That's the good thing about his gun compared to Mick's. It folds down small and he can fit it into his schoolbag.

'Out past Smith's?' I say.

He looks at me and smiles, like he's trying to fix things between us.

'Sounds good,' he says.

•

Smith's Caves aren't really caves but a group of massive rocks on the edge of town. Our teacher told us that Aboriginal people used them for shelter, but then some bloke named Smith found them. That's why they're called Smith's Caves. We learned about it on an excursion.

I don't know why they're called caves and not rocks either. At least Margaret's Hill is actually a hill. Whoever she was, she got that right.

Out behind the rocks there's mostly scrub, which is full of snakes, then empty paddocks where nothing seems to grow. Danny says it's Crown land, which means you're allowed to go shooting there.

His dad told him the Queen of England owns it, and she could come and live there if she ever wanted to. I don't reckon she'd ever want to, though. It's dry, ugly, and full of mixos. And it's not far from the tip, so it stinks when the wind's blowing the wrong way. Beside the Crown land is Blind Gully Forest, but we never go in there.

We hide our bikes behind the rocks and start walking. None of us have brought any lunch, so we decide we'll just stay out for the morning. Chadwick has five bucks that he's sposed to use at the canteen, so we agree that we'll go to Greasy Pete's after, buy three corn jacks, and spend the rest on chips. Corn jacks are kind of like Chiko Rolls, but full of mashed corn. They're salty and really delicious.

It's pretty incredible that Chadwick has five bucks just for lunch, but I don't say anything. I don't want to make a big deal of it, not in front of him.

Greasy Pete's has Galaga as well, so we might have enough left over for a game, depending on who's working. If it's Greasy Pete, he'll charge full price. But his daughter, Tracey, always gives me a discount. She even gives me stuff for free sometimes, especially if Sam's with me.

Tracey's older than us, but not by much. She's in high school, but only year seven. She works at lunchtime most days, just to help Greasy Pete with the till. Especially since Mrs Pete got sick with cancer. Greasy Pete's is actually called The Hungry Fisherman, but no one calls it that. It's been Greasy Pete's forever.

Chadwick hasn't got a gun, so Danny gets him to carry his shovel instead. Danny always takes a little shovel, like a gardening one, because he reckons if we find a good warren, he could dig it out. But rabbit warrens are really deep and the ground out here is dry and hard. The one time he tried to dig one out, he gave up pretty quick.

Danny walks out front, with me and Chadwick a few metres behind. Danny always carries a stick in case there's any snakes around. He also has a coil of rope over his shoulder, a bit like Charlie's, just in case one of us falls down a mineshaft. But if one of us falls down a mineshaft, I don't think the rope will be much help.

I remember Mick saying once how a mineshaft would be the perfect place to dump a body. I heard him saying it to Travis Greenwood. I don't know how he'd know, but I spose it makes sense. They go a long way down, and no one would ever think to look there.

The sun is starting to get warm, and I feel like I should say something to Chadwick. Just to break the ice a bit. He's too quiet, and it feels awkward. When you don't know someone very well, the quiet is much louder.

'How long you had that bike?' I say.

'Since Christmas.'

'Mongoose, isn't it?'

'Yep.'

I listen to our steps crunching through the dry grass. Danny walks ahead, looking all serious with his stick and rope.

'My bike's pretty crap,' I say.

He nods.

I try to think of something else to say.

'Have you wagged before?'

He shrugs.

'Will you get in trouble?'

He frowns. 'What for?'

'For wagging. If we got caught.'

He shakes his head. 'Nah, Mum wouldn't care.'

'Really?'

'Yeah.'

Danny stops up ahead. He turns back and holds a finger to his lips.

'Shhh,' he says.

He points to a small hill of dry weeds and bare earth up ahead. Maybe fifty metres away. There's a few rabbits there, not moving much.

'They're just mixos,' I say.

Danny nods. 'Yeah, but better than nothing.'

'What's a mixo?' Chadwick says.

Danny's eyes narrow, like he's about to explain something important. 'It's when they've got myxomatosis. It's like a disease.

They're poisonous for humans, so they're no good for eating, and they go all slow and stupid.'

Me and Danny get our guns out of our bags and load them. You only get a single shot each time with the slug gun, and it's the same with Danny's air rifle.

I've killed a few birds with the slug gun before, mostly sparrows. Once I got a magpie. I felt bad after, so I don't shoot birds anymore. But I've never killed a rabbit, and neither has Danny. Only Tippy got one once, before he died. We never get close enough before they run off. And if it's windy, the slugs get blown off course. That's what Danny says, but I reckon we're probably just bad shots.

We creep up as slow as we can, until we're about twenty metres away.

'Shhh,' Danny says, even though no one is saying anything.

The rabbits definitely look like mixos. They're moving really slow, like they haven't even seen us.

Danny starts to bring his gun up to his shoulder. I put my fingers in my ears. I glance at Chadwick, who has this worried look on his face. I wonder if he wishes he hadn't come.

Crack!

The gunshot is much louder than Danny's air rifle, and he hasn't even aimed yet. The rabbits scatter. The sound echoes for ages, and my ears are ringing.

Danny crouches down.

'Shit!' he says. 'Someone's shooting.'

I look behind us toward Smith's Caves but can't see anyone. 'Sounds like a twenty-two,' I say. 'Or a three-oh-three.'

We stay down, not moving.

'Maybe it was from the rifle range,' Danny says.

'Maybe,' I say. 'Should we keep moving?'

Danny nods.

We walk toward the patch where the rabbits had been. Grass seeds catch in my socks and they're rubbing on my skin. I would've worn my woollen socks, but they've gone missing. I got them at Christmas because Mum got them from her work for free. I wondered if she might've stolen them, but I didn't say so. I got the socks at the same time Chadwick got his Mongoose.

I thought it was probably Sam who took my socks, so I told him off for it. Then I felt bad. That's the thing about Sam, you always feel bad if you tell him off. So I try not to.

It's hard sometimes with him, but there's good bits too. Like how I can talk to him about stuff, and he always listens. He's a really good listener, even if he doesn't say much. Sometimes that's enough.

.

We didn't get any rabbits. But we still go to Greasy Pete's for lunch after, like we planned. It's pretty busy with some council workers, and Tracey is working the till while Greasy Pete sweats over the hot plate and fryer.

Tracey has her long black hair in a ponytail with a pink scrunchy, and the pimples around her mouth look worse than normal. She has a pale blue school uniform on under her apron.

'Hi, Jimmy,' she smiles. 'Day off?'

'Yep.'

'Where's Sam?'

'School.'

'He's going okay?'

'Yep.'

She smiles again. 'That's good.'

We don't get the corn jacks. Danny says three potato cakes and three dim sims is better, because we can share them out. We get chips too, but there's still enough left over for each of us to have a game of Galaga.

Tracey is careful with the till, so her dad doesn't see her giving Chadwick a discount.

'Thanks,' I say.

She smiles at me, and I feel my face going hot.

Danny is pretty crap at Galaga, and so am I. Chadwick is the best by miles. He says it's because he has it at home.

'Seriously?' Danny says.

Chadwick has his eyes on the screen, fingers moving fast across the buttons, almost like he could do it in his sleep.

'Yeah, on the computer. An Amiga. Got it for my birthday.'

Me and Danny look at each other. We've seen the ads on

telly for the Amiga, but didn't know anyone who had one. Not till now.

'Why didn't you show us?' I say. 'When we came round?'

Chadwick shrugs. 'Didn't think of it. It's in the computer room.'

'We should come over again then,' Danny says. 'So you can show us.'

Chadwick's face glows in the blue-green light.

'If you want.'

Chadwick finishes with the second-highest score. It doesn't let him put his whole name in, so he just writes LUK. It takes him ages to scroll through all the letters, but it's still pretty impressive. Galaga has been at Greasy Pete's forever.

We leave not long after. But first we decide we'll go to his place again in the next few weeks, especially if the weather's good, so we can use the pool as well.

I like the idea of having a go at his Amiga. Especially if Mrs Chadwick is there, and especially if she makes us lunch again.

SIX

There's two lakes near Mittigunda – Lake Brownville and Lake Redfin. Redfin is the good one.

It's full of water most of the year, and it's where the Sunnyvale Caravan Park is. Sunnyvale is where tourists from the city go, sometimes even people from overseas. That's what Danny tells me.

Some people from town stay there too, when they have holidays. They don't stay at the other caravan park on the edge of town. The one where Charlie lives. It's called The Meadows. There's no lake at The Meadows, not even a dam, and it's mostly people living there for good, not just for holidays.

Danny's family stay at Sunnyvale when they go to Redfin, which is how I know about it. He reckons people come from all over Australia, and some even bring speedboats and jet skis, like the ones you see on *The Price Is Right*. They've even got a shop out there, but it's only open in summer.

'It's like the milk bar,' Danny said. 'Only smaller and really expensive.'

Brownville is the other lake. I've only been there with school. We went there for two nights and stayed at the scout camp, which was okay. There's no caravan park. I really missed Mum and Sam when I was there. Mick was in jail, so I was used to not seeing him. I really missed Tippy too, even though he was dead by then. I remember the toilets stunk really bad, because they were long drops.

I tried not to be homesick, but it was hard. I kept thinking about all the things that could go wrong while I was gone. Like if Sam got sick, or Mum died, or if Mick got stabbed in jail. The second night was easier, mainly because I knew I was going home the next day.

Lake Brownville doesn't have as much water as Redfin. If it hasn't rained in a while, you can walk right across it. Mick promised to take me and Sam there once or twice, but he never did. He said he preferred it over Redfin.

'Aren't as many people,' he said. 'It's more private.'

He used to go camping with Smelly and Travis Greenwood at Brownville. I think they went with girls too, because I heard him and Smelly talking about some girl named Kylie one time.

I've never known Smelly's real name, because everyone's always called him that. He doesn't seem to mind, though. He has long blond hair down to his shoulders, and he's kind of goofy looking. He drives a yellow ute with extractors. Extractors make an engine sound really loud, much louder than it actually is. His is the only car in town that has them, and it has tinted windows too. He bought it with money he'd saved working at the abattoir, because he left school for a really good job as a meat boner.

He's right into his fishing, and he's always been pretty nice to me and Sam. He isn't quiet and serious like Travis Greenwood was. Mick is probably somewhere between the two. In being serious, I mean.

The thing I don't like most at Lake Brownville is the trees. There's old dead trees in the water, about fifty metres out, and they look like skeletons. They're standing up like normal trees, but they're grey and dead and have no leaves. I don't know how they grew out there, but I don't like going near them.

Mick reckons there's fish near the trees, mostly yellowbelly and trout. Smelly goes out there in a tinny when they're camping.

The water at Brownville is dirty too, but not as bad as a dam. Even so, there's heaps of sticks and stumps you can bump your feet into.

All in all, it's a pretty crap lake. But when Mum told us that Charlie was going to take us there, I was pretty excited. It's good to be going somewhere for a change, and it's pretty nice of Charlie to take us.

•

On Friday night, Mum told us we'd have to be in bed by nine because Charlie wanted to leave early. The Kingswood wasn't running, so he'd borrowed a car from a mate.

I hope he'll have the Kingswood going again by the time Mick gets out of jail. Maybe we can pick Mick up like we did last time, in Aunty Pam's car. But I won't say anything about it because I don't want to jinx it.

Mum said Charlie is getting all the camping gear ready at his place. She said we don't need to pack anything except our clothes, and anything we want to play with.

'He'll look after everything else,' she said. 'Even the food.'

It's pretty good of Charlie. And Mum looks pretty happy about it all.

I wonder if Charlie has ever thought about changing caravan parks, if he'd move from The Meadows to Sunnyvale. It'd be better out there, but probably more expensive.

One of the things I don't like about The Meadows is the sign out front. They painted the sign on the two big septic tanks near the gate. It's not so much what it says, or how it's painted, but that it's painted on septic tanks. They should've put the tanks out back somewhere, not right at the entrance.

We've only been to Charlie's cabin at The Meadows once, and it was really small. It smelled like plastic and cigarettes, even though he had an ashtray out the front.

He had a poster of the Richmond Football Club from 1980 stuck on the wall with sticky tape. One of the players had laces up the front of his top, like from the olden days, even though it's only six years ago.

Charlie seemed really nervous when we were there. He stood up nearly the whole time, and kept moving things around in his little kitchen, like he didn't know what to do. I'd never seen him like that before. There was nowhere really for me and Sam to sit, so we sat on the bed. It was squeaky and soft.

He made me and Sam a Milo, and him and Mum had a tea. I couldn't wait to go home. I think he was a bit embarrassed about where he lived, and I felt a bit sorry for him.

•

It's hard to get to sleep so early, mainly because I can hear the telly on in the lounge room. It's *Prisoner*, which is one of Mum's favourites. Her other favourite is *Sons and Daughters*. That show is incredibly boring. Everyone is always looking stressed, having arguments, or having long conversations on the phone. Most times, she watches *Sons and Daughters* on the little TV in her bedroom. *Prisoner* is heaps better, even just the sound of it.

I open my eyes to the dark of our room, and there's a small glow from underneath the door. I listen to Sam breathing softly in and out, but I can tell he isn't asleep yet.

'Wish we were going to Redfin,' I say.

Sam rolls over and the bunk squeaks. He's getting bigger, and I wonder if one day he might come crashing down on top of me.

'Hear me?'

'Hmm?'

'I said I wish we were going to Redfin tomorrow.'

He sighs.

'We've never been there. It's the good one, where rich people go.'

He takes a few deep breaths in and out, then rolls back toward the wall. I hear the music start up on the telly in the lounge room, the sad roses song. It makes my heart hurt a bit. It always makes me think of Mick.

I wonder what he's doing, and if he's still awake. He usually stays up late, so I think he would be. He's probably reading the magazine I sent him, the one I got from the newsagent. I saved up some of my change from the Craven A's to get it, instead of getting mixed lollies. It was *Wheels* magazine. It's all about cars, so I thought he'd like it. It had the latest Commodore on the front, and it was painted bright orange. It was a custom job, I think. I don't think you can get them in that colour.

What I said to Sam isn't completely true. It isn't just rich people that go to Lake Redfin. Danny's family isn't rich, and they still go. But it's mostly people who are well off. People like

Chadwick. They go on holidays every year at summertime, while the rest of us stay at home and pretend.

I don't mind, though. Staying at home and pretending, I mean. It's definitely better than being at school.

But the bit I don't like is when we go back to school after the holidays, because that's when the other kids talk about what they did. That's the worst bit, because you don't have much to say. Nothing, really.

Sam starts snoring, and I close my eyes and hope for sleep. I hope it comes soon, so the morning will too, and we'll be going on a holiday for once.

A camping trip. The first time in ages. Even if it's just at Brownville.

•

Charlie picks us up after breakfast. He beeps his horn out front, but it's much louder than a normal horn.

'Quick, you boys,' Mum says. 'Don't want to keep him waiting.'

The car is unbelievable. It's a black Falcon GT, with a green racing stripe down the bonnet. Mick would love it, and I wish he was here to see it.

Charlie hangs his arm out the driver's side window, taps the door. He has a big smile on his face and I can tell he's proud, even if he's just borrowed it.

'Your chariot awaits,' he says.

Mum's wearing a yellow summer dress, which I've never seen before, and I can see she has her swimmers on underneath. The dress makes her look younger, a bit like the pictures I've seen in the photo album.

'Check it out,' I say to Sam. 'I think it's a V8.'

We get in the back seat like usual, with me on the right and Sam on the left. Mum sits in the front. Charlie whispers something to her and she laughs. He reaches over and touches her thigh.

'Not in front of the boys,' she says. She made it sound like she was telling him off, but she smiled when she said it.

'Thanks for taking us, Charlie,' I say.

He eyes me in the rear-view. 'My pleasure, mate. What do you think of the wheels?'

'Cool,' I say. 'Really cool.'

Charlie laughs. 'I'll tell Bluey that. Bit showy for my taste, but she rocks along.'

He starts it up and reverses slowly out of the driveway. The engine sounds incredible. I can feel it rumbling in my bones, and I decide it's the best car I've ever been in, maybe even better than Mick's Pacer. I can't wait to tell Danny about it.

Charlie turns up the radio once we hit the highway, and it's the song where everything she does is magic. Mum starts singing along, then Sam starts humming too.

Charlie doesn't sing, but he taps the steering wheel. I close my eyes and listen, and feel the sun warming up my skin.

•

Charlie is really good at setting up camp. He has folding chairs, a table, and a big tent made from heavy green canvas.

'Done a bit of travelling, this one,' he says. 'All the way to Saigon and back.'

He sets it up mostly by himself, a fair way back from the sand and under a gum tree. It's a good spot. It's in the shade, but close enough to the water without getting sand in everything. He gets me and Sam to hold the corners of the tent while he nails the pegs in. I think he could have done it himself, but just wanted to get us involved. I can tell Sam is concentrating really hard, like he wants to do a good job. Charlie notices too.

'Great work, Sam,' he says.

Once the green tent is up, Charlie puts up a small cream-coloured one for me and Sam. It's a bit further back from the water than the green one, and it's shaped like a teepee. I like it. He does it on his own, so me and Sam just watch. It takes about half the time of the green one.

I wonder how Charlie got so good with camping stuff. Maybe it was in Saigon. He never talks about Vietnam much, but I know he went there for the war. Mick told me. He said it's why Charlie doesn't work much.

'It fucked him up a bit,' he said. 'In the head.'

He tapped his head when he said it, in case I didn't get the message. But I don't think there's anything wrong with Charlie's head, so I wonder why Mick said it.

Mick also said that Charlie was a sniper. I heard him say it to Travis Greenwood.

'A freak with a rifle. Killed heaps of Viet Cong.'

I don't know how he could know that, though. I don't think Charlie would have told him, but maybe he did.

While Charlie was doing the tents, Mum set up a table and chairs on the tarp Charlie had spread out over the ground near their tent. He put it there so we wouldn't get sand in everything. She got the esky and barbecue out from the boot of the GT. The barbecue is a little fold-up one that Charlie brought. He brought everything, and almost everything is fold-up. Somehow, it all fitted in the boot of the GT, like it was the Tardis from *Doctor Who*. I've never liked that show much, it's scary, but Mick always watches it. The worst is the Daleks.

I notice Mum is wearing the gold necklace Nan gave her, which she hardly ever wears. And the big fancy sunglasses she bought from the chemist. They're made by Le Specs, like in the ads on TV. She looks a bit like a movie star.

.

Once everything is set up, we have a game of cricket. Mum doesn't play, so we make her scorer. Sam doesn't really play sport, but he has a go at batting. Charlie calls him Viv Richards, and himself Trevor Chappell. Charlie bowls underarm to him, and Sam manages to hit a couple. We all cheer like crazy.

'Nice shot,' Charlie says. I run as slow as I can after the ball, so Sam will make the run back. Mum is clapping like mad for him.

One of the best bits is that there isn't anyone else around. Mick was right about that. It's like we have our own private beach, like we're on a desert island. There might be other people, but I can't see them. I look out across the lake, to the trees on the other side, but I can't see anyone. So I decide it's just me, Mum, Sam and Charlie. The only thing that would make it better was if Mick was here.

When things are happy like that, it can make you sad about what's missing. Like Mick. And Nan. Tippy too. He would've loved running around on the sand like a mental case while we were playing cricket. But I'm not sure if Charlie would've let him come. He never liked Tippy very much.

I dunno if Mick would've played, or even if he would've come, but I like to think he would've. When I see him again, I'll tell him he was right about Brownville. It's better than Redfin. You don't have to worry so much about what other people think.

Even when things feel good, the happy times are never completely happy. I'm not sure if it's like that for everyone. It's not like in the movies, or on TV, where some people are just happy without ever being sad. Maybe when you're older you get to be happy all the time. But when I think about Mum, and about Mick, I know that can't be true.

The sun is starting to get warmer, and Charlie starts to get puffed.

'Let's have a breather,' he says. 'Viv's running us ragged.'

He takes off his t-shirt and I see more tattoos up his arms. They're green too, but I can't read them either. His chest is really hairy, but some of the hair in the middle is white. He lights up a smoke.

'Might have a swim after,' he says. 'If it keeps warming up.'

I really hope we don't.

•

Once we finish with cricket, me and Sam decide to go for a walk around the lake. Mum tells us not to go too far. She gives us a honey sandwich each to take with us. Honey sandwiches are Sam's favourite. I used to like them when I was younger, but not as much now. Mum still likes to make them for me, so I don't say anything.

We stop under some trees a little way from our campsite and eat our sandwiches. There's heaps of birds around. Flies too, which is annoying. We share a juice, but it isn't very cold. It's my favourite flavour, though. Orange and mango.

After lunch I wade into the shallow water. I only go a bit past my knees, because I'm worried it could get too deep. Plus,

I don't want to get my shorts and undies wet. Mick says there's bits of the lake where it gets deep quick, and you can't tell just from looking.

Sam watches me from the sand. I try to get him to come in, but he won't. It starts to get cold, so I get back out. I haven't brought a towel, but the sun dries me pretty quick.

We find some big sand dunes a bit further on, and I wonder where all the sand came from.

'They must bring it here from the beach,' I say. 'In trucks or something.'

When we get to the top of the dunes, I roll down like a barrel. Sam starts clapping. I do it again, but end up with sand in my shorts.

When we get back to camp, it's probably about four o'clock. It's hard to know the time when you're on holidays, and even harder when you're camping. Charlie starts laughing when he sees me.

'It's Lawrence of Arabia!'

I don't know what he means, but Mum laughs too. She gets me to go in the water and rinse out my shorts and undies. It's pretty embarrassing. I face away from the camp so Charlie won't see.

Charlie gets the barbecue going for dinner not long after. It feels like it's early for dinner, because it's still really light, but I think time works different when you're on holidays.

Mum sets up the table with the plastic plates and cups. They aren't normal cups, though. They're coloured steel ones, and they look amazing. They're different colours – red, green, gold and blue. I want the gold one, but I decide to wait until we sit down to see which one I get. They're Charlie's cups, and I don't want to take his favourite by mistake.

'Do you want any help, Mum?' I say.

She shakes her head. 'Not much for us to do out here. Not with the chef in charge.'

Charlie smiles, and I feel warm inside. For once, it feels like everything is going perfect.

'Did you and Sam have a good walk?' Mum says.

'Yep.'

'Might go myself tomorrow morning, before we head back home. If you boys are still keen?'

'Yep,' I say. 'Definitely.'

Charlie cooks sausages and forequarter chops, plus some onions and potatoes. I'd hoped we were having hamburgers, but the chops and sausages still smell great. The onions too. Forequarter chops are probably my favourite chop, because of the round bone in the middle. The meat in the bone is always really tasty. But it takes Charlie a while to cook the meat.

'Blasted burner isn't working properly,' he says.

I've never seen Charlie cook before. He even has an apron on, a denim one, with blue and white stripes. He finishes the potatoes and onions, then scrapes them to one side of the hot plate.

While the meat is still cooking, he gets a little radio from his tent. It takes a while, and he has to move it to a few different spots, but he manages to tune in some music. There's a fair bit of static, but it's okay. He catches me watching him, and I feel embarrassed.

'Grab us a beer, Jimmy.'

I fish a stubby from the esky. The ice has mostly melted, and I have to reach a long way down, past my elbow. It's really cold and my arm goes numb. I get his stubby holder from the table, push the beer inside, then pass it to him.

He winks at me. 'Good lad.'

My face goes warm when he says it.

Charlie normally drinks cans, but he says the bottle shop only had stubbies. The stubbies won't stay as cold as a can, which is why he brought his stubby holder. He only ever drinks the white cans, Carlton Light. He says he prefers Victorian beer, because he originally came from there. It's hard to get in Mittigunda, but the bloke at the bottle shop looks after him.

Mick told me that Charlie only drinks light beer because of the problem in his head. The one he got in Vietnam. But I don't know if that's true.

Mum gets the salads out of the esky and takes the Glad Wrap off. She's been drinking a bit of the Kaiser, and I notice Charlie watching her. It's good someone else is keeping an eye on her and the Kaiser, because it's a lot of work on my own. Especially since Mick went to jail.

I hadn't realised she'd brought the Kaiser. If I'd known, I wouldn't have gone for a walk with Sam. I would've stayed by the campsite and kept watch. Because once she starts, it's hard for her to stop. Nearly impossible.

I don't think Charlie likes Mum drinking too much, and I don't like it either. Mum's old boyfriend Keith drank even more than she did, which I think made her drink extra too.

Mick didn't like Keith much. Probably even less than he likes Charlie. One time, him and Keith had a big fight and Mick bashed him pretty bad. It happened after Mum had stopped seeing him, but Mum was still pretty upset about it.

Bashing Keith was part of the reason Mick went to jail this time, but not the whole reason.

.

Before he went to court, Mick was worried he was gonna go inside. He didn't know for sure, not a hundred per cent, but his lawyer said it wasn't looking good.

Mick's lawyer was from Legal Aid, which means you don't pay much. His name was Robert Goldthorpe. I had to stay home with Sam, but Mum went to court with Charlie and Mick. They went in Charlie's old ute.

Mum said he was hopeless. Robert Goldthorpe, I mean. She said Travis Greenwood had a better lawyer, one from Sydney.

Mum said Mrs Greenwood had put the milk bar up as surety to pay for him, but I wasn't sure what that meant.

The day before sentencing, Goldthorpe told Mick to 'prepare himself', but Mick didn't really do anything different, apart from get his duffle bag out from under my bed.

I was lying in my bedroom reading the *Footrot Flats* I'd borrowed from the library. I wasn't allowed to borrow any more, because I hadn't taken that one back and it was overdue. But I'd wanted to read it one more time. It has an excellent cover with the Dog protecting Jess from Murphy's dogs, but not realising the cat, whose name is Horse, is right behind him.

It was hard to concentrate on the story with Mick reaching around under my bed. In the story, the Dog was trying to keep warm in his kennel, which is really just an old water tank. It was raining a lot because it was winter. It's nearly always winter in *Footrot Flats*. The Dog was still in the tank, but the water outside was rising up around him.

Eventually, Mick found the bag. He stood up.

'Stop reading for a sec.'

His eyes looked a bit shiny, and I wondered for a second if he might cry. It must've been my imagination, though, because I've never seen Mick cry. Not even once.

'You know I'm going back inside, right?'

I shook my head.

'The lawyer reckons it's not looking good, mostly because I've been slotted before. And because of what happened with Keith.'

'Okay.'

The time before was for burglaries. It was the same this time. But now they had him for the assault too.

'Make sure you look after Sam, yeah? And be good for Mum. But watch out for Charlie.'

I didn't really know what he meant about Charlie.

'Yep,' I said.

Even though I tried to be good, Mum got worse with the Kaiser after Mick went to jail. But I'd never tell him that. Then she got worse again when Nan died. She hasn't been working as much since then, but I don't know if it's because of the Kaiser, or because she's sad. Maybe both those things.

I try to be good at home, and at school, so she'll feel better. If she feels better then maybe she won't drink as much. But it's been harder to make her happy since Mick went to jail, even when I'm extra good.

She usually starts in the afternoon, and she goes slow at first. Then she gets faster.

'The Kaiser's my only friend,' she said once, and I've never forgotten it. It was the day after Mick went to jail, and she'd been drinking really fast. She doesn't have many friends, apart from Aunty Pam. And Aunty Pam is her sister, so I'm not sure that counts. Nan was her friend too, but she's dead.

I don't think the Kaiser really is her friend, probably the opposite. She likes to drink the Kaiser, but sometimes the Kaiser drinks her too. It's hard to explain. It's like it takes part of her to somewhere else. I can see it in her eyes, because they look like they're seeing something I can't see.

The only thing I like about the Kaiser is the silver bag inside, because I like blowing them up. Sam loves it too. We use them as cushions on the couch, even if they're noisy and not very comfortable. If you squint your eyes, the cushions make the couch look like it's from the future, or from outer space.

That's the only good thing about the Kaiser.

•

It turns out that Sam gets the gold cup I'd wanted, and I get the red one. The red one is still really nice, though, and the chops and the sausages are delicious. Mum even made a special coleslaw salad, which she hardly ever does.

'Thanks for cooking, Charlie,' I say.

He smiles. 'A pleasure, mate.' Charlie looks at Sam, but he doesn't look up from his plate. 'I think the salads were the star of the show,' Charlie says.

'Thanks, Mum,' I say. 'They were really delicious too.'

Mum has taken her sunglasses off, and her eyes are looking at the place the Kaiser shows her, but she isn't there yet. Not completely. She's still mostly with us, so I have to be extra good to keep her here.

It's starting to get dark, so Charlie turns on the camp light.

'How about we go watch the sun go down over the lake,' he says. 'Should be a ripper.'

We pick up our folding chairs and carry them down to the sand. I go back and get Sam's. The sky is looking beautiful and pink near the horizon.

Charlie takes the radio down to the sand too. He gets some better reception, so turns it up a bit louder.

'Ah, here's our favourite.'

I can tell straight away it's Dolly Parton singing, because I've heard it about a million times. It's the 'Islands in the Stream' song.

Charlie gets up and takes Mum's hand. She tries to shake him off, but I can tell she doesn't mean it. She's smiling and he's smiling too. She stands up and they both start dancing. It's so embarrassing.

Charlie sings along to the Kenny Rogers bit, and Sam starts clapping. Mum takes his hand and the three of them dance in a circle. I feel my face going red, even if there's no one else around, but I can't help smiling a bit too.

Mum holds out her hand to me.

'C'mon,' she says. 'You too.'

I shake my head. 'Nah, I'll just watch.'

I try not to smile too much. When things are good like that, you don't want to jinx it.

•

Once the sun goes down, everything goes quiet. Apart from Sam's humming and the insects. There's suddenly hundreds of them around the camp light. They're mostly moths, but there's mozzies too.

Charlie had given me a torch, but when I turn it on it just makes more of them come, so I turn it off again.

Charlie and Mum are sitting at the table drinking, but he's slowed down a bit. He's watching Mum even more than before. I don't know how much she's had, because I can't check it. They aren't talking as much, though.

After a bit, Charlie gets up and tries to change the radio station, but he can't find another one. Then he can't find the one he had before.

'Fuck it,' he says.

I can feel something changing. It's mostly in the air between him and Mum. It isn't like before, down near the water at sunset. It's different. It's a bit like the time he pushed her.

Sam starts humming again. Charlie gives him a look and says, 'Cut it out, mate.'

Calling him mate doesn't make it sound any nicer. I can tell Charlie's angry, even if he tried to make it sound better in front of Mum.

Mum looks a bit drunk. The corners of her lips have curled, and her eyes have gone thin, which means she's mostly at the other place. I shouldn't have gone off with Sam in the afternoon. I should've stayed and kept an eye on her and the Kaiser. The Kaiser is sneaky, and if you don't keep an eye on him, he'll find a way to ruin things.

The mozzies start getting really bad, so I decide to head for the tent.

'Goodnight, Mum,' I say.

She gives me a sleepy smile, and I smile back as best I can.

'Goodnight, Charlie,' I say.

'Night, Jimmy.'

He doesn't look at me when he says it. He must be annoyed with me. I head for the tent.

'C'mon, Sam.'

I turn on the torch to lead the way.

.

It feels small inside the tent, but nice too. When Charlie set it up, he rolled a foam mattress out, and two sleeping bags. Me and Sam are on the same bed, but separate.

Sam gets into his sleeping bag and falls asleep pretty quick. I'm tired, but I lie there and listen for the sounds outside. I have to listen to make sure everything is okay with Mum and Charlie. I can hear the water lapping from the lake, and the wind in the trees. I can feel it getting cooler, so I pull the sleeping bag up to my chin.

I stay awake for as long as I can, but I can't hold on forever.

SEVEN

I wake up to the low rumble of the GT. I unzip our tent and poke my head out. The sun is just starting to come up, and the air is still cool.

I see the car reversing slowly from the campsite. Charlie's driving, and he spots me. He stops, keeps the engine running, and waves me over. I walk across the campsite, twigs poking into my feet. He winds down his window.

'Morning, Jimmy,' he says.

'Morning.'

'Sleep okay?'

'Yep.'

'That's good. I was worried the mozzies might've bothered you. Listen, I just gotta go see a mate. Won't be long.'

'Okay.'

He's angry, but he's trying to hide it. I can tell from his face, and from the air around him. He's still upset because I went off with Sam in the afternoon. That I left him to watch Mum and the Kaiser all on his own.

'I'll see ya a bit later on,' he says.

'Yep.'

He reverses back out onto the dirt road, then swings the GT away from the campsite. I'll try to look happy when he comes back. I'll tell him how much I've liked the camping trip so far, especially the game of cricket and the cooking. Then he'll know I was sorry, and things can go back to how they were.

I'll never make that mistake again. I'll make sure I keep an eye on Mum, especially if the Kaiser is around. It's too much for one person.

•

Once Sam gets up, I decide to go to Mum's tent. It's zipped up tight. I try to listen, try to hear if she's still asleep.

'Mum?' I say.

She doesn't answer.

'Mum?'

Nothing.

'Me and Sam are ready for our walk. Remember?'

I wait for a bit. She must still be asleep. She usually sleeps for longer after the Kaiser. That's what I tell myself.

I take Sam down to the edge of the lake. It's cooler than yesterday, the sun hidden behind some clouds. There's more wind too. I try skimming some stones, but the most I get is three skims. Sam has a go, but only gets two. The water is grey and choppy.

'I wish she'd get up,' I say.

Sam looks at me.

'If Charlie comes back and she's still in bed, he'll get angry.'

Sam picks up another stone.

'I wish she wouldn't drink so much.'

It's the first time I've ever said those words, even if I've thought them heaps of times. It feels good to say them out loud, but bad at the same time. I felt angry at her when the words came out, but then sorry for saying them. You can feel a lot of things in just a few seconds.

'I better go wake her,' I say. 'So she's up when Charlie gets back.'

I leave Sam by the water and I go to their tent. A magpie starts warbling somewhere in the trees above.

'Mum?' I say.

The zip is at the top, and it takes a bit of effort to get it loose. When it won't move, I notice there's a button underneath, holding it in place. Maybe she couldn't get out.

Once I get it open, I can smell something sweet.

'Mum?'

It's much darker inside their tent than ours, and it takes a while for my eyes to adjust. But I can see her shape, on her side on the mattress. She's facing away from me.

'Mum?'

I go closer, and the sweet smell is stronger. I listen for her breathing, but I can't hear a thing. I kneel down beside her. Her head is half covered by the blanket, her face in the pillow. I touch her shoulder. Her skin feels cold.

'Mum?'

She lets out a breath.

'What?'

Her voice is all croaky.

'Are you getting up?'

I notice her black bra on the floor, the lacy one I've seen on the clothesline. She's probably nude under the covers, and I can feel my face going red.

'In a minute,' she says.

'Okay.'

I go outside, zip the tent up as best I can. Sam is still down by the water, trying to skim stones.

It's longer than a minute, definitely. Time is like that sometimes. It can go fast, like on school holidays, but it can go really slow too. It's usually when things aren't good.

When she finally comes out, she's dressed in her black jeans and a blue flannel shirt. Her hair is messy, and she staggers a bit. She looks away from me, but I can tell she knows I'm watching. She moves slowly. She shields her eyes and looks to where the car was, then up the dirt road.

'Get my sunglasses, Jimmy.'

'Where?' I say.

'On the table.'

I do what she says, and it's when I give them to her that I see. Her left eye is all swollen and bruised.

I feel a pain in my guts, my chest, then my throat. I want to cry, but I hold it in.

'Mum?' I say.

She takes the sunglasses, gives me a look. I know what the look means, because I've seen it before. It means don't say anything, so Sam doesn't get upset. So he doesn't run away like last time. Don't say anything, so we can just pretend.

She puts on her Le Specs, but I know the truth. I know what's underneath. It's like the last time when Charlie pushed her against the wall, only worse.

'Everything's okay, Jimmy.'

I feel sick. I didn't stop it from happening. I should have been better.

'I'm sorry, Mum.'

'Shhh,' she says. 'Sam's coming.'

Sam is walking back from the lake, carrying stones in his hands. When he gets close, he shows them to me.

'They're good ones,' I say, but my voice is croaky. 'Good for skimming.'

He smiles with his eyes, and Mum smiles too.

And I realise she's right. It's easier to pretend, it's better that way.

•

We pack everything up quick once Charlie gets back. I try hard to pretend I'm not angry with him, but it's hard. It's really hard to pretend. Much harder than with Sam.

Part of me wishes Mick was out of jail. Part of me wishes he might do something bad to Charlie, maybe even worse than he did to Keith. Something to teach him a lesson.

Charlie and Mum didn't talk once he got back, and they've barely looked at each other. It was like it'd already been decided. There wasn't time to walk around the lake, and I didn't ask.

The drive home is quiet. No one talks, and the air is thick between Mum and Charlie. Mum looks out her window like she never wants to look at him again. She's even worse at pretending than I am.

Once we get back on the highway, Charlie tries to put the radio on, but it's mostly static. We're still too far from town. After a bit, he tries again and gets something. It isn't Dolly

Parton, though. It's someone singing about a ring of fire, and the man's voice is rough and deep.

After we take the turn-off back to town, I see someone walking up ahead beside the road. It's a girl in blue jeans and a pink jumper. She has a backpack on, her thumb out.

'Hitchhiker,' Charlie says.

Mum doesn't say anything.

Charlie puts the indicator on, and starts to slow down. Mum turns toward him.

'Is this a joke?' she says.

'What?'

'Where do you think she'll sit?'

'We'll squeeze her in the back with the boys. Probably just wants a ride into town.'

'If she gets in, I'm getting out.'

When she says it, it's like all the air in the car gets sucked out. It's hard to breathe. I'm scared Mum is going to get out of the car, and then she'll have to walk all the way home. I'm scared she'll get lost, or something bad might happen to her. Something even worse than what Charlie did.

Charlie shakes his head.

'Just fucking forget it,' he says.

He turns the indicator off, and accelerates past the hitchhiker. I try to see her face when we pass, but we're going too quick. She would have been disappointed. She had long black hair, and I wonder where she was from, and what she was doing all the way out here on her own.

Sam starts humming. I reach across and take his hand in mine. I smile, but he doesn't smile back. Not even with his eyes. He must know my smile isn't real.

The next camping trip will be better. I'll be extra careful, and I won't make any mistakes. I'll stay with Mum the whole time so nothing like that can happen again. I'll be happy to go to Lake Brownville, and I won't complain about it to Sam, or even to myself.

Those things can make a difference sometimes. Even the things you're thinking, even if you don't say them out loud.

I'll be better next time. I'll get everything perfect.

PART TWO

ONE

Every Monday we have PE with Mr Battista. He's always really nice. Before he was a PE teacher, Mr Battista played footy for Essendon in the reserves. He only played a few games, though, before he did his knee.

His nickname when he played was 'Whisper'. That's what Danny told me. Mr Battista is pretty quiet and he never yells, so we've decided that's the reason.

We played rounders this time, which is one of my favourites. It's like baseball, but with a flat bat. I'm pretty good at it. Usually, I'm one of the first picked, after the sporty kids.

I use one hand to hold the bat, like a tennis racquet, because I can hit it further that way. But I can't really concentrate this time.

I'm still thinking about what happened with Mum and Charlie. After Charlie dropped us home, he sped off in the GT like a race car driver. The tyres were squealing and everything. It was like something from the James Hardie 1000, or from a movie. Mrs Simpson was out gardening in her front yard and she saw the whole thing.

Mum has stayed in her room pretty much the whole time since, and it makes me worry. She didn't get up for breakfast, so I had to get Sam ready for school. It made me late, so I missed the start of rounders.

I'm still really upset at Charlie for what he did. He shouldn't hit a girl, and he definitely shouldn't hit our mum.

At the end of the game, after we pack everything up, Mr Battista says he has an important announcement. Everyone goes quiet, because when teachers say that, it's usually pretty big news. Like an excursion or something. I'm worried it might be about the swimming carnival, because we're definitely due to have it. It's always at the end of summer, not long before Easter.

'The school is doing something it's never done before,' he says. 'For the first time, we're having a billycart race.'

I look at Danny, and he looks at me. This is going to be the best thing that's ever happened at our school. That probably isn't saying much, but still.

'It'll be an annual event from now on,' Mr Battista says, 'With a trophy for the winner.'

He tells us anyone in the school can enter, apart from the preps, but there'll be two separate divisions. Because we're in grade five, that means we'll be in the same division as the grade sixes and grade fours.

'You'll have to do a lot of training if you want to win.'

The full rules will be put up on the school noticeboard next week, and he says that each team will have three members. Two to push, one to steer.

'You'll need to organise yourselves into teams,' he says.

He also says the course will be on the oval, and there's no downhill section, so we'll have to be really fit to push the cart.

'It'll happen in exactly one month.'

I listen as carefully as I've ever listened to anything at school, maybe anything in my whole life. The whole class is quiet right through, but then the talking starts. You can tell everyone is excited, even the girls. You can feel it.

David Knight puts his hand up to ask a question.

'What about the swimming carnival?' he says.

I know why he asked. David Knight is the best swimmer in the school, even better than the grade sixes. He represented our school at the district championships last year, but he didn't win.

'Thanks, David,' Mr Battista says, 'I was coming to that.'

I'm not the only one who hates the swimming carnival. Melissa Dowling can't swim either, but she usually gets out of it with a note from her parents. Even so, she looks as worried as me.

'We've changed the date of the swimming carnival to the second half of the year. It'll be in November. They've got some maintenance work to do on the pool, so the timing's good.'

It's the best news I've heard in ages. Both the billycart race and the swimming carnival. November is forever away, and anything could happen before then.

Danny grabs me by the arm. I can tell he's really excited.

'Have you got a billycart?' he says.

'Yeah, but it's old. And I'm not sure I'm allowed to use it.'

'Why not?'

'It's Mick's.'

'How's he gonna know?'

'He's getting out soon.'

'When?'

'Soon.'

'You've been saying that for ages.'

Danny's like that, he never takes no for an answer. And the truth is, I don't know exactly how much longer Mick has got in jail. The last time I asked, Mum said it wasn't long. That was ages ago. But the look on her face made me feel like I shouldn't ask again. Like it reminded her of the bad things he'd done.

Sometimes I wish Mick would come home right away, especially after what happened at Brownville. Charlie probably wouldn't have hurt Mum if Mick had been there, but I don't know that for sure.

Anyway, I know there's no point thinking about it. Wishing Mick was home isn't going to change anything. And if Mick was home, there'd be other problems.

When he's in jail there's less to worry about, even if I miss him sometimes.

But the billycart race is the perfect way to make things better. If we win, it'll make Mum happy. And Mick will be really proud when he finds out. It might fix a lot of things, all in one go.

Danny wants to come over straight after school and start training.

'Nah,' I say.

'Didn't you hear Mr Battista? We'll need to be fit.'

'I have to pick up Sam from the bus stop.'

'After then.'

I do have to pick up Sam, but that isn't the real reason I don't want him to come. The real reason is because of Mum. I don't want Danny to see her eye, because then he might tell his mum, and then people will talk. Mum doesn't like it when people talk. People like Mrs Simpson.

But I know he won't take no for an answer.

·

Veronica is on Sam's bus, smiling like she always does. Like every day is the greatest day ever. Neville is there too, but he's asleep with his head against the glass.

Don brings Sam carefully down the steps, holding his hand. He keeps the engine running, and it splutters a bit like it's about to stall.

I catch Sam's gaze. He smiles with his eyes.

'G'day, Jimmy,' Don says. 'Where's your mum?'

'At work,' I say.

I take Sam's hand. It's sticky. Don eyes me.

'She's been going okay?'

'Who?'

'Your mum.'

'Yep.'

He scratches his chin.

'What about Charlie?' he says.

I feel my face getting hot.

'He's still coming round?'

'Yeah.'

He nods, crosses his arms.

'You've been okay?'

'Yep.'

'School all right?'

'Yep.'

His questions are making me nervous. It's like the more he asks, the less I can hide things. He knows something, but I don't know what. Maybe people are talking already. Maybe Mrs Simpson has told him about Charlie speeding off, or about Mum's eye. I decide to tell him.

'There's gonna be a billycart race.'

His eyes go wide.

'Billycart race? Is that right?'

'Yeah.'

'At school?'

'Yep.'

He gets this big smile.

'We're gonna use Mick's billycart. Me and Danny. It's a bit old, but it should be okay.'

Sam squeezes my hand. Don's still smiling.

'That's great, Jimmy,' he says.

'Yeah. I don't think Mick'll mind us using it.'

'Wouldn't think so. But if you need a hand getting it ship-shape, let me know.'

The bus splutters again.

'I used to be a mechanic, so I know my way around vehicles. Even high-performance ones.'

'Okay,' I say. 'Thanks, Don.'

He reaches over and roughs Sam's hair. Sam flinches, like it annoys him, but I can tell he likes it.

Don climbs the steps. Once he's back in his seat, he calls out.

'Say hello to your mum too, Jimmy. From me.'

'Yep,' I say. 'I will.'

•

The Firefox is in the shed out back. It was named after a Clint Eastwood movie with jet fighters that Mick saw at the drive-in. I wasn't allowed to go. He went with Smelly and Travis Greenwood instead.

The billycart is mostly made of wood, but has a plastic seat screwed into it. Mick stole the seat from Frank Jenkins' front yard and took the legs off. The wheels were from a couple of bikes he found at the tip. The back ones were from a racer, and the front ones off a BMX. There's just a rope to steer.

I helped him make it, but I was young then. It was a woodwork project he had to do at the Tech School, and he'd left it to the last minute.

I liked watching him put it together. I liked passing him the tools. I thought it was pretty incredible he could build something like that, all by himself. He painted the name down the side in silver paint, and it looked amazing.

But it isn't how I remembered.

It's covered in dust and *The Firefox* letters look all wobbly, like a little kid painted them, or like Mick didn't know how to write properly. I feel embarrassed for ever mentioning it.

'It's not too bad,' Danny says.

'Maybe once we clean it up,' I say. 'It'll look better then.'

He shrugs. 'Maybe.'

'Don reckons he can help.'

'The bus driver?'

'Yeah. He says he used to be a mechanic.'

We carry it out of the shed, down the driveway, and onto the footpath. Sam follows. Mum's inside, in her bedroom, and hasn't come out since we've been home. I know she's in there, because I listened at the door. I could hear the little TV.

Sam's been quieter than normal since what happened at Brownville, since he saw Mum's eye. He's mostly stayed in our bedroom and played with his Rubik's Cube.

Danny puts his arm around him.

'Wanna be our driver?' he says. 'When we win, you'll be famous.'

Sam doesn't answer, but I know he can't do it.

'Who we gonna ask?' I say.

'For our third?'

'Yeah.'

Danny shrugs. 'Chadwick?'

I get on the seat and grab hold of the rope. The seat is hard and uncomfortable on my bum. Danny starts pushing, but the wheels are flat.

'We'll have to get them pumped up,' I say.

'Let's give it a go anyway.'

Thing is, I've only ever driven *The Firefox* once before with Mick, and it was down Margaret's Hill. It really flew, or at least that's how I remember it. I remember Mick yelling at me too, because I was terrible at steering.

Danny gives it another shove, but we go nowhere. Sam runs down the footpath ahead of us, and Danny pushes harder.

I tug the rope to turn the front wheels straight, and it starts moving. Like the time with Mick, I'm having trouble keeping it straight. Sam starts clapping. Danny keeps pushing, but he's out of breath in no time.

He starts laughing.

'We've got no hope,' he says.

'Once the tyres are fixed, it'll be better.'

TWO

After school on Friday, Mum makes me and Sam a toasted cheese and tomato jaffle. It's the first time we've had one in ages. It's boiling hot, but really delicious. I make Sam wait for his half to cool down, so he doesn't burn his mouth on the tomato.

Mum sits at the table and watches us eat. She must've gone to the supermarket while we were at school, because the fridge has more stuff in it. There's a new Kaiser too, but it hasn't been opened. The spout is still inside the box, and I hope it stays there for a while.

Her eye is looking better. The swelling has gone down, and the purple went red, and then the red started to fade. It's good because she can go out, and good because the reminder of what happened isn't there all the time.

Charlie hasn't been around. I wonder if him and Mum might have broken up. I hope so, but I'm not sure how to ask.

She puts the telly on, and we sit on the couch because it's time for the cartoons. It's *Roger Ramjet*, which is one of Sam's favourites. He starts humming.

After it's finished, *Inspector Gadget* starts up. Mum clears her throat.

'How was school today?' she says.

'Good,' I say.

I want to tell her about the billycart race, but I should wait for the right time. You should save good news for times when you need it.

We go quiet for a bit. Inspector Gadget is hunting diamond smugglers in the land of tulips and chocolate. I've seen it before.

'Charlie might be coming over later.'

She says it quiet, but loud enough for me to hear.

I try to hide what I'm feeling. I look at Sam, but he's staring at the telly. I don't think he heard what she said.

'I know what happened was scary,' she says. 'But he's said he's sorry. And he's promised it won't happen again.'

I try to hold my feelings in my chest.

'He's really promised this time.' She pulls the hair away from her face, back over her ears. 'I've told him it's his last chance.'

I'm pretty sure he promised last time too, but it's no good saying it. Maybe she can't remember, or just doesn't want to.

'Okay,' I say.

It's the opposite of how I feel.

Mum turns the volume up on the telly. It's the same song at the end of *Inspector Gadget* as at the beginning. I'd felt good at the start, just after the jaffle, but at the end I feel completely different.

I keep looking at the telly so she can't see my feelings. That's the best way.

'You'll understand better when you're older, Jimmy. People are complicated.'

Maybe she can feel it in the air, like I can with her and Charlie.

Sam starts humming again. Mum changes the channel to *The Littlest Hobo*, which is another one of Sam's favourites. It's about a dog who travels around from town to town, getting in adventures. It makes you feel sad and happy all at once. The dog is free and does what he likes, but it's sad because he's all on his own. It reminds me of Tippy, which makes the sad part worse. The song at the start is probably the saddest bit.

'He's gonna help out more too,' Mum says. 'With bills and the groceries. Things like that. Especially now they've cut my hours at StormShield.'

I know she hasn't been going to work as much, but I didn't know they'd cut her hours. It's not good when she isn't working as much, because it means more time for the Kaiser.

Maybe she's taken too much time off, and they got sick of it. Or maybe they found out about her stealing the woollen socks. I would have been happy without them. Next Christmas, I'll tell her I don't need a present.

'I'm really sorry about what happened, Jimmy.'

She squeezes my arm and smiles. Seeing her smile, and her eye still red like that, it almost makes me cry.

'It's okay, Mum. It wasn't your fault.'

She puts her arm around my shoulders and gives me a hug. I close my eyes and make a wish. I can't say what it is, or it won't come true.

THREE

On Saturday, we go to Chadwick's. This time, it's hot enough to have a swim, so we don't end up playing with the Amiga.

'We'll save it for winter,' Danny says. 'We can use it then.'

I notice how he's talking about Chadwick's stuff almost like it's his own.

I'm a bit nervous about the pool, mainly because I don't want to look stupid. Even though Danny knows I can't swim, and I think Chadwick might too, it's still embarrassing.

Sam stays inside with Mrs Chadwick. She asked if he might like to swim too, but I told her he can't, which is true.

It's good how Mrs Chadwick is looking after Sam. She seems to like him, which is nice. It's always been me, Mum and Danny who spend the most time with him, apart from the other kids at the Special School. Maybe Charlie too. And Mick, before he went to jail. And probably Don the bus driver. But that's really it, so it's good there's someone else now.

When Nan was alive, she loved seeing Sam. It's still so sad that she died, and I wonder if that feeling will ever change. She always said she wasn't going to be around forever, but it still seemed really sudden. I wasn't ready for it, but maybe she was.

When she died, the people from The Oakview rang Mum to tell her. Mum was really upset. She cried for a long time, then she went to the nursing home. She didn't talk much for a few days after.

Sam was really sad too. He was more quiet than normal for a few weeks. Most people wouldn't notice, but I did.

I think Nan loved Sam the most out of us boys. She'd get him to come sit beside her at the nursing home, and she'd pinch his cheeks. She loved him more than anyone in the world, I think, apart from Mum. And she told me I had to look out for him.

'Make sure you do, Jimmy.'

That's what she said.

It's been a while now since she died, but sometimes it still feels like she's alive. Like if I went to The Oakview, I'd still see her there, sitting in her room with her telly up too loud. I could sit beside her bed, and she could tell the same stories to me, over and over, and I wouldn't mind one bit.

People never really disappear. Not completely, I don't think. A part of them is always left behind.

•

The pool is in the backyard, next to the lawn. There's a low brick fence around it, but no gate or anything. Danny reckons it's the only in-ground pool in town, apart from the public one, but I don't know how he can be sure.

It's about ten metres long and surrounded by smooth, grey cement, with bright blue tiles at the edge. The cement is really hot, so it feels nice to dangle my feet in the water.

I wonder if Mick has a pool in jail. The first time he went inside, he told me they had a small one, but they didn't get to use it. That was the youth prison, which is sposed to be nicer than the adult one he's in now.

Chadwick and Danny muck around at the deep end, doing bombs to see who can get the biggest splash. I spread out the towel Mrs Chadwick gave me, then climb slowly into the shallow end. I walk in about halfway to where the water is up to my chest. It's cool, but not freezing.

The pool is pretty narrow, so I think I might be able to get from one side to the other. I try swimming underwater, pushing myself off the wall to the other side. I keep my eyes open while I'm under, and the chlorine stings a bit, but it's nice and quiet and clean under there. It feels like nothing can touch me. It's peaceful. There's just the hum of water and the bubbles in my ears.

After a bit, I sit back up on the edge of the pool. I let the warm sun dry my skin. I dangle my feet back in, but it doesn't feel as cool anymore. I go back to the towel and lie down. It's soft and thick, not hard and dry like the ones at home. I close my eyes and listen to Danny and Chadwick splashing and laughing. A lawnmower starts up somewhere, and there's the clicking noise from the filter thing at the end of the pool. I can hear birds too, but I don't know what they are. Not magpies or plovers or anything like that. One calls out, then another answers from further away. When you close your eyes like that, you can hear more things.

Danny and Chadwick eventually get sick of doing bombs, and decide to have a race. Four laps. Danny hasn't shown me anything about how to swim like he promised, but I don't care that much.

Danny makes me umpire. They both stand at the far end and wait for me to start. Danny has this look on his face like it's super serious, but Chadwick looks pretty relaxed.

When I say 'Go!', Chadwick dives in like a professional. Like something you'd see at the Olympics. Danny jumps in feet first.

Chadwick goes through the water like a snake. His white skin slips through the pool like he was born to do it. He's hardly even puffing by the end.

When Danny eventually finishes, he coughs up a bit of water. A thin line of snot runs from his nose to his lip. He lost by a whole lap.

He takes a while to catch his breath. Then he says that Chadwick had an unfair advantage.

'He's got a pool, so he can practise.'

It's a fair call, but I reckon even if Danny had a pool, he would never beat Chadwick. He just doesn't have the right body for it. He's too stocky. Chadwick might not be good at most sports, but it seems like swimming is his thing. He probably isn't as good as David Knight, but not far off.

After the race, Chadwick and Danny do some more bombs, until they get sick of it, and then they float on their backs. I put my elbows up on the side of the pool and try to get my legs to float, but it doesn't work. Even so, it's nice to be in the water. I like the feel of it, and how being underwater made everything so peaceful.

It's really quiet for what feels like ages. Then Danny says, 'How come your dad's never home?'

Chadwick takes a while to answer.

'He works a lot. And they argue when he's here.'

'Really?' Danny says.

'Yeah. That's why Dad doesn't come home much. Because they just fight all the time.'

'What about?'

'Dunno. Everything really.'

We all go quiet again, and there's just the lapping of the water and the slow clicking noise from the filter thing at the end of the pool.

Then Chadwick says, 'I don't think they love each other anymore.'

I've never heard anyone say anything like that before, apart from in movies, or on the shows Mum watches on telly. I look across at him. He's still floating on his back and staring up at the sky. It's like he wasn't talking to anyone in particular, and it wasn't very important, and he was just telling the whole world about it.

I wonder if I should say something, but I can't think what.

After what feels like ages, Danny says, 'Fair enough.'

The sun goes behind a cloud. I start to get cold, so I pull myself out of the water. Chadwick decides to get out too, even though Danny wants to do some more bombs.

While we're drying off, Danny asks Chadwick about the billycart race.

'You in a team?'

'Nah, not yet.'

'Wanna be in ours?'

Chadwick looks at me, then Danny. It's like he's unsure. Maybe Bradley Whitehead or Stephen Murphy have already asked him.

'You two?' he says.

Danny nods. 'Jimmy's got a billycart.'

'Yeah? What's it like?'

'Bit crap.'

I feel a sting in my chest. Even if it's true, it annoys me that Danny said it.

'It's not that bad,' I say. 'And Don is gonna fix it. He was a mechanic.'

Chadwick puts his t-shirt back on. It's a Rip Curl, dark blue with thick yellow stripes.

'I've got one,' he says. 'A billycart, I mean.'

Danny looks surprised, but I'm not sure why. Chadwick seems to have everything, so there's no reason he wouldn't have a billycart too.

•

The garage is at the end of the driveway, and it's huge. It's about the same size as our house, but made of brick. It's dark and cool inside, and there's stuff all along the walls. There's two golf bags, a folded-up table tennis table, and a surfboard. Basically everything, and it all looks nearly brand new.

But the main thing is the cars. Two BMWs, exactly the same. One's red and the other's black.

'Wow,' Danny says. He walks beside the cars and stares like they're the best thing he's ever seen in his life.

'Pretty nice,' I say. 'Why two the same?'

Chadwick shakes his head. 'They're not the same.' He walks around the front of the black one. 'This one's a turbo.'

Danny's eyes are like saucers. 'A turbo? Can I get in?'

'Nah, don't touch them. My dad cracks it if anyone goes near them. They're just for weekends. He uses the four-wheel drive, mostly.'

'They're both his?' I say.

'Yep.'

'What about your mum?'

He shrugs. 'She's got the station wagon.'

Chadwick's dad has a black moustache and looks a bit like Magnum PI. I saw a picture of him in the rumpus room the last time we came over. Magnum drives a Ferrari, though, not a BMW. And he's only got one.

We follow Chadwick to the back of the garage. In the corner, leaning up against the wall, is the billycart. But it doesn't really look like a billycart. It's more like a miniature version of a car, without doors or a roof. Like a car stripped down to its skeleton. Like a dune buggy, but without an engine.

It's made of steel, and has a leather seat and roll cage. It's almost like something from *Mad Max*. It even has a proper steering wheel.

'Jesus,' Danny says. 'It's better than yours, Jimmy. No offence.'

I want to say something to stick up for *The Firefox*, but without sounding like a sook. Me and Mick had done our best when we made it, and Mick had no one to show him. Plus, he'd done it all in just one day. That's what I want to say, but I can't think of a clever way to say it.

You only ever think of the best things to say later on, when it's too late to say them. Sometimes never.

Chadwick and Danny start talking about training. Danny says we could have a real shot. Even though the grade six boys are bigger, Danny doesn't think any of them will have a cart like Chadwick's. Not one with a roll cage and proper steering.

'It's rack and pinion,' Chadwick says. 'My dad made it.'

I don't know what rack and pinion is, or how his dad knew how to make it if he's a lawyer. I wonder if Don might know how to make something like that, and if he could put it on *The Firefox*. I doubt it.

Chadwick and Danny decide I'll be the driver, because I'm the smallest, and they're both faster runners.

'What do you think?' Danny says.

'Yeah,' I say. 'Sounds good.'

Chadwick's cart probably does give us a better chance of winning. And if we win, things might get better. Winning is probably more important than using *The Firefox*.

We take it out front for a test run along the footpath. It's pretty incredible. It's like driving a dodgem car at the carny, only faster, easier to steer, and you don't have some weirdo hanging off the back of it.

Mrs Chadwick comes out and watches us going up and down the street. I like that she's watching, and I hope she's impressed with my driving. She goes back inside for a bit, then comes out with Sam, plus three cans of Coke.

We stop and drink the Coke. It's icy cold and delicious. Mrs Chadwick gets Sam to sit in the billycart while we're having a break. She gives it a push. Sam starts humming, so she stops right away.

'It's okay,' I say. 'That means he likes it.'

She smiles and keeps pushing him down the footpath. Sam keeps humming and starts clapping too, so the cart starts going in all directions.

Mrs Chadwick has no shoes on and her skirt is blowing in the wind. She's laughing and Sam is still clapping. And just for a minute, I forget about Charlie, *The Firefox*, and everything else.

FOUR

We decide we'll practise at the resi the next Saturday. Like I said, the reservation is its proper name, but no one calls it that.

Danny says we have to start early, first thing, so we'll have plenty of daylight. We're meant to meet at Chadwick's first, to get the cart, so me and Sam have to leave even earlier to get there on time.

Mum's still asleep, so I'm as quiet as I can be. I help Sam get dressed.

'Shhh,' I say. 'Don't wake Mum.'

'Okay.'

Charlie has been around a couple more times during the week. I've made sure I'm there the whole time, to keep an eye on things. It's been okay so far. He's being extra nice to me and to Sam to make up for what happened at Brownville, to make us forget. He did the same thing after the last time, when he pushed her. It doesn't work, not completely.

Once we're outside, the air is cool and the sun is still low in the sky. I can hear the hum of cars and trucks on the highway in the distance, carried by the breeze. A dog barks, another barks back, and the birds are starting to call to each other. It feels like the town is slowly waking up.

When we turn onto Franklin Street, I hear someone calling out. At first, I can't tell what they're saying. But then I realise.

'Jimmy!'

I squeeze Sam's hand and turn around.

Don's standing in his front yard, up near the fence. He's wearing a light blue dressing gown, and has a rolled-up newspaper in one hand. His hair is white and all messed up, like he's just gotten out of bed.

'Morning, Jimmy. G'day, Sam.'

'Morning, Don.'

He smiles, and I see a few of his top teeth are missing. He covers his mouth with his hand, like he's embarrassed. I feel bad for him. He must wear false ones when he's driving the bus.

'Where you boys off to?'

I shrug. 'Meeting some friends.'

'Fair enough. Pretty early for it, mind you.' He taps the front fence with his newspaper. 'How's things going with that billycart?'

I suddenly remember his offer to help with *The Firefox*. He doesn't know we've decided to use Chadwick's, but it feels too complicated to explain.

'Good,' I say.

He taps the fence again with his newspaper.

'I can take a look if you like. Got a bit of time. Plus, my back's not giving me grief. For the moment, anyway. Have you done any work on it yet?'

I shrug.

'Check the bearings?'

'Nah.'

He shakes his head.

'Well, that type of thing makes a hell of a difference. You'd be surprised.'

I can see his pyjama pants showing below his dressing gown. They're red stripy ones, old-fashioned. He has old-man slippers on, tartan ones, and it makes me think of Nan.

I want to keep going to Chadwick's, but I don't know how to end the conversation. I look past him to the house, and see there's a light on inside. I hope like anything his wife will call him in for breakfast. I can hear a car coming from around the corner. I look down the street, wondering if it might be Charlie coming over. Then I remember his Kingswood still isn't running.

'Okay,' I say. 'You can have a look.'

He smiles, covers his mouth again.

'Beauty. Bring it by next weekend. I'm always here.'

•

The resi is on the edge of town, and it's a big block of land full of gum trees, but with narrow walking tracks that snake right through it. Some kids use it for BMX racing, or to meet for fights instead of at the Tech School. It's a good spot for training, even if it's a bit of a hike, because there's hardly ever anyone around.

'So no one sees us,' Chadwick said. 'So we'll take them all by surprise.'

Chadwick and Danny walk ahead with the billycart, with me and Sam behind. Sam is going slow, which makes me go slow. He holds my hand tight.

'Mick'll be home soon,' I say.

He nods.

'Next few weeks, I reckon.'

It's just a guess, but I know it's been over a year since he got sent inside. His sentence was sixteen months, so I figure it can't be long now.

A bird starts whistling in a tree in the nature strip as we pass. There must be a nest. Sam stops and looks for it.

'It'll be good when he's back,' I say.

'Yep.'

The bird flies out from the tree, and it looks like a honeyeater.

Sam smiles. He likes birds. It'd be great if we could get a bird as a pet one day. Sam would love it.

Chadwick and Danny go further ahead, but I can hear them talking about the West Indies cricket team, about their favourite player. It's a conversation me and Danny have had heaps of times, and I'm pretty tired of it.

I'm not that into sport, but I still like watching the one-day cricket if the West Indies are playing. Even so, it's good Danny has someone new to talk to about it.

I squeeze Sam's hand.

'Things are gonna get better, you know?'

'Yep.'

'Once Mick gets out. And once we win the race.'

'Okay.'

'So we've just got to be good till then.'

'Yep.'

'If we're good till then, Mum won't drink as much of the Kaiser. Then Charlie won't hurt her. Things'll be different.'

By the time we get to the resi, the sun is getting warm. I help Sam take off his windcheater and I tie it around my waist.

In the middle of the resi, there's a pond that's dried up. That's the spot where people usually meet for fights. Even though there's hardly ever any water, there's some tall reeds growing in the middle. When it had water, me and Danny used to catch tadpoles sometimes, but then we got too old for it. Sam used to watch us, so I know he likes that spot.

'You wait here,' I say. 'We'll do a bit of practice, then we'll come back. Won't be long.'

I open my bag and give him the Rubik's Cube. He has three sides done, the blue, the green and the white.

To be honest, billycart training is pretty easy for me, because Chadwick and Danny have to do all the work. Both of them are pretty stuffed by the end. I just have to steer, and that's heaps easier than with *The Firefox*. Maybe because it doesn't have the rack and pinion.

Chadwick reckons we're a really good shot of beating the grade sixes.

'We could win the whole thing.'

Danny found out from Mr Battista that there's gonna be obstacles on the course, some hay bales and ramps.

'Battista reckons it isn't just about speed,' he says. 'So we'll have to be careful taking corners. But because this thing is easy to steer, we should have an advantage.'

Chadwick smiles, and Danny does too. I think they're both imagining what it'll be like if we win.

When I think about it, a warm feeling fills me right up to the brim.

•

After we've practised for a while, Danny says we should go to the milk bar.

'Get some drinks and mixed lollies,' he says. 'For energy.'

'Nah,' I say. 'I'm not hungry.'

Truth is, I'm starving. I just don't have any money.

Chadwick is keen, though. He gets Sam to sit in the billycart, then pushes him the whole way. He goes slow, but I have to reach over Sam's shoulder sometimes to steer because he keeps working on his Rubik's Cube.

Me and Sam wait outside the milk bar with the billycart. I didn't want Sam to go in, because sometimes he grabs stuff off the shelves without asking.

'Sure you don't want something?' Chadwick says.

'Nah, I'm right,' I say. 'Thanks, though.'

'What about Sam?'

'Nah,' I say.

Chadwick nods. 'Righto.'

Sam stays in the billycart. He has half the yellow side done, but he's messed up the green side in the process.

'Nice work,' I say.

He gives me a look.

When they come back out, Chadwick hands me a Golden Gaytime. He sees the look on my face.

'It's no worries,' he says.

He gives Sam a chocolate Big M. I know he prefers strawberry, but I don't say so.

'Thanks,' I say. 'From both of us.'

.

On the way back to the resi, Danny says we'll need to give the billycart a name.

'*Firefox Two*,' I say.

Danny laughs, and it annoys me a bit.

'How about *The Interceptor*?' he says. 'Like the car in *Mad Max*.'

'Nah,' I say. 'Too obvious.'

The Interceptor is an excellent name, because it does look like something from *Mad Max*, but I want to get him back for laughing at my idea.

'Maybe we should get Sam to name it,' Chadwick says.

Danny laughs, but Chadwick looks like he means it. He stops and crouches down in front of the billycart.

'What do you reckon, Sam? What should we call it?'

Sam's eyes go down. I can tell Chadwick looking at him up close like that is making him uncomfortable. He stops playing with the Rubik's Cube.

'He doesn't like when people get too close,' I say.

Chadwick stands up.

'Sorry.'

I shrug. 'That's okay.'

Chadwick scratches his head. 'How about *Quiet Sam*. Maybe that's what we should call it.'

Danny screws up his face. 'Seriously?'

'Yeah.'

It isn't a name I would've picked, but it's pretty nice of Chadwick to think of it. And there's something special about the way he said it too. Something in his voice. It's hard to explain, but it makes me feel warm inside.

Quiet Sam.

'It's a good name,' I say.

FIVE

Charlie has been coming over even more now, like Mum said he would. I don't like it, but things have been better than before. Better than Brownville, definitely.

This time, he's brought fish and chips from Greasy Pete's, and Mum makes a big deal of it. He's brought a big bottle of lemonade too. It's good he's brought the fish and chips, and Mum seems happy, but I don't like seeing him much. I feel a bit scared of what might happen.

Even so, the fish and chips are delicious. He puts vinegar on his chips, which I've never seen anyone do. I try some, but it's sour and horrible.

Charlie laughs when he sees my face.

'I can see how much you like it.'

He's brought fish and chips over once before, and it was on a Friday too. I don't really want to talk to him, but I feel like I should say something. Something that makes it seem like things are more normal again.

'Do you always have fish and chips on Fridays?' I say.

He eyes me. My heart beats hard in my chest, and I wonder if he can see my thoughts.

'Sometimes,' he says.

'Why?'

'Because I'm a good Christian.'

Mum laughs, so I laugh too, even though I don't really know what I'm laughing at. Things are like that with grown-ups sometimes. It's better to just play along like you understand, even when you don't.

Even if we're laughing, and things have been better, I hope Charlie knows it's his last chance. He's trying extra hard, but it doesn't work. Not for me.

'Maybe we should go fishing sometime,' he says.

'Yeah?' I say.

'Yeah. Up in the hills. I know a creek full of blackfish. You have to do it at night, though, so we'll camp for a couple of days. Just you, me and Viv Richards.' He gives Sam a wink. 'We'll have a cricket rematch too.'

'Okay,' I say.

'Give your mum a bit of a break.'

I feel scared at the idea of camping with Charlie on our own. Being out in the dark, up in the hills. Especially without Mum.

'Blackfish are the best,' he says. 'Beautiful, sweet flesh. Not like this stuff.'

I wonder why we have to do it at night, but I don't ask. I wonder why he didn't invite Mum too. Mum looks at me, and I can tell she wants me to say something.

'That'd be good,' I say. 'Thanks, Charlie.'

I feel a bit sick when I say it, and the words make my throat feel sore.

After we eat, him and Mum watch telly together on the couch. The Kaiser is on the kitchen bench, but Mum only has one glass. They watch *Dynasty*, which is incredibly boring, but it's also one of Mum's favourites. That and *Dallas* and *Sons and Daughters*. All three are terrible. I stay up and watch, but Sam goes to bed.

After it's finished, Charlie does a big stretch.

'Better head home,' he says.

Even though he said he should go, he takes ages to leave. I wonder if he's hoping Mum might ask him to stay. I really hope she doesn't. After a bit, he stands up and gets his jacket.

'Thanks for the fish and chips,' I say, but I don't really mean it.

He smiles. 'No worries, Jimmy. Least I could do.'

Mum goes to get up, to show him out, but Charlie tells her to sit. Then he says he'll be away for a bit.

'Off shearing the next couple of weeks.'

'Oh,' Mum says.

Charlie looks at me and winks. 'So you're in charge while I'm gone, Jimmy.'

Mum gets up and they go outside together. She's gone for ages. When she comes back in, she pours a glass of the Kaiser. She drinks it fast, refills it, then sits back down on the couch.

The Kaiser looks happy, like it's part of the action again. I sit next to her, where Charlie had been. It's still warm in his spot.

The Dave Allen show is on telly. Dave Allen is Irish and he's always drinking whiskey, and part of a finger on his left hand is missing. His show is mostly him telling jokes that I don't really get. Mum is watching without really watching, I can tell. When the ads come on, she gives my arm a squeeze.

'Did you have a good night?'

'Yep.'

She nods. 'Me too. It's good he's got some work again, though. Means we'll have some extra cash for when Mick comes home. We can all go out for dinner. To celebrate.'

'Really?'

'Yep.'

I smile. 'That'd be good. Does Charlie have to come?'

'To dinner?'

'Yeah.'

'I haven't even told him Mick's coming back yet.' She looks at me and frowns. 'But you don't want Charlie to come?'

I feel my face going red, and I wish I hadn't said it. I should've just kept pretending. Dave Allen is back on the telly, and he's telling a joke about a priest, but Mum turns it down.

'What's up, Jimmy?'

'Nothing.'

'C'mon, you can tell me.'

The tears come to my eyes. I wish they didn't. I wish I could've kept them in, but sometimes it's impossible.

'I don't like it when he hurts you.'

She puts her arm around me, pulls me in close. She's warm and I can feel her breath going in and out. We stay like that for ages.

'It's all right,' she says. 'It can just be us at dinner, then. Just me and you and Sam and Mick.'

It makes me glad when she says it, the thought of it. I wipe my cheeks.

'Sorry,' I say.

'It's okay. Things will be better once Mick gets home. You'll see.'

I swallow, and my throat hurts.

'When's he getting out?'

She reaches over to the coffee table, gets a cigarette, lights it. The smoke fills the space between us and the telly. I like the smell.

'Hopefully soon. He's due for parole, but it'll depend on when the meeting is scheduled. And if he's behaved himself.'

She looks at me, then takes another drag.

'Parole is where the prison decides if he can get out early, but it depends on a lot of things. Like if he's been getting in trouble or not, and if he's been doing the programs.'

I can't really imagine Mick not getting into trouble, but I don't say so. I'm not sure exactly how the programs work either, but I guess it's probably something like school, which Mick was never really interested in.

Mum finishes her smoke, butts it out in the ashtray.

'Even if he gets parole, he'll have to behave himself once he's out. Otherwise, they'll send him back.'

It doesn't sound like it's going to work. Knowing Mick, even if he gets out on parole, he'll be back inside pretty soon. It sounds like a bit of a trap to keep him in jail forever.

But maybe it'll be different this time. Maybe he's done the programs and he'll be better.

Maybe people can change, or at least pretend to. Just like Charlie.

SIX

When I agreed to take *The Firefox* to Don's, I didn't think it through. I was just desperate to get to Chadwick's.

After one weekend went by, I thought he might've forgotten. But when he dropped Sam off the following Friday, he reminded me.

'You right for tomorrow?'

'Tomorrow?'

He smiled. He had his bus teeth in.

'The billycart, remember? I was home last weekend, but you must've had other things on.'

'Sorry. Must've forgot.'

'No worries. It's not like I had anywhere to be. I'm around tomorrow, though.' He shrugged. 'If you still want to, of course.'

I should've told him about Chadwick's billycart right then, about *Quiet Sam*. It was the perfect time. But I thought he'd be disappointed. When you know what it feels like, you don't want anyone else to feel it.

'Okay,' I said. 'That'd be great.'

•

Danny cracks it when I tell him.

'We're sposed to be training,' he says. 'We've only got two weeks left.'

'Sorry.'

'You should've just told him about Chadwick's billycart.'

Even though we've named it *Quiet Sam*, Danny never calls it that. It annoys me a bit. I think he's still upset we didn't call it *The Interceptor*.

'Why's he so keen to help?'

'Don?'

'Yeah.'

'Dunno.'

'You sure he's not a perve?'

'Nah. People can just be nice, can't they?'

•

Mum's still in bed, so I make toast in the morning for me and Sam. There's no jam left, so we just have margarine. It's nice on its own sometimes, especially if you eat it when it's still warm.

Sam points at the telly.

'We can't. It'll wake Mum.'

I want to get to Don's early, because I told Danny we'd still be able to train in the afternoon. I said I'd meet them after. That way I can keep Danny happy, and make Don happy too.

After breakfast, we walk to Don's place in Franklin Street. Sam pulls *The Firefox* by the steering rope all the way there. It's slow going. We stop at the front gate. In the driveway, there's a blue Toyota Crown.

'Wait here,' I say.

I open the gate, cross the front lawn, and go up to the porch. The floor of the porch is speckled concrete, and there's a brown security door with a doorbell beside it. I press it, but I can't hear anything inside. I wait a few seconds, then press it again.

Maybe Don forgot, or had to work. Or maybe the doorbell's broken.

I knock on the security door and it's loud and rattly. A few seconds later, I hear footsteps inside. When he opens the door, he seems out of breath.

'Sorry, Jimmy,' he says. 'Was just out back.'

He's wearing dark blue overalls, the bib ones, with a white shirt underneath. In the top pocket of his overalls is a pencil. It's a thick one, like I've seen builders use.

'Where's Sam?' he says.

'Out front.'

Don steps past me.

'Morning, Sam. C'mon up!'

I can smell pine trees in the air around him, a bit like the shaving cream Mick uses sometimes. It's fresh and clean smelling.

Sam opens the gate and pulls the billycart inside and around the front of the Crown. He gives Don a funny look, almost like he doesn't recognise him. Like he might only know him when he's driving the bus.

'Great to see you, Sam.' Don pats him on the shoulder. 'Come in, come in.'

The hallway is much darker than I expected, and the air smells like dust. The floor creaks almost everywhere you step. There's brown stripy wallpaper, old-fashioned, and it's peeling off in a few spots high on the wall. I can see cracks underneath.

'Come through,' he says.

The lounge room has a couple of armchairs, but no couch. There's a TV in one corner that looks even older than our one. A big window looks out to the neighbour's wall.

On the mantlepiece, above the gas heater, there's a photo of a couple on their wedding day. They're in front of a church, standing on the steps. It looks a bit like a young version of Don, but with blond hair. It must be Mrs Don with him.

He sees me looking.

'Big day, that one.'

I nod.

'Come out back. Got something for you both.'

The kitchen is at the back end of the house, with a round wooden table in the middle. It's sunnier there. One chair is steel and blue vinyl, and it doesn't match the two wooden ones.

In the centre of the table is a square fruit cake, still in the red box it came in. It's the Lions one. The ads are always on telly near Christmas time, but it's ages till Christmas.

'Sit, sit,' Don says.

I help Sam sit on the vinyl chair, and Don fills the kettle. The kitchen is like something from the olden days. There's an old white stove, and the cupboards are cream coloured, but with pale blue doors.

Don switches the kettle on, and it starts to hum.

'Jeez, where's my manners?'

He gets a knife from the drawer, takes the cake out of the box, then cuts three thick slices. I wonder where Mrs Don is.

'Butter?'

'Yes, please,' I say.

Even though we've already had breakfast, I don't want to disappoint him.

Sam starts eating his slice.

'Wait, Sam,' I say.

Don smiles.

'If you're hungry, just start,' he says. 'I remember what it's like at your age. I was always bloody hungry.'

The kettle boils, and Don makes himself a cup of tea. He

sits down on the chair beside me. A clock ticks loudly on the wall, and seems to get even louder when everyone is quiet.

'Thanks for the cake,' I say. I take another bite. It's rich and sweet and fruity, just like the ads say on telly. 'Really nice.'

He smiles. 'Pleasure, Jimmy. Good to have some company.'

Sam wolfs down his slice, so Don cuts him another. I notice the wallpaper in the kitchen is different from the rest of the house, with pale green stripes. I wonder if maybe Mrs Don is somewhere visiting friends. Or maybe she's out shopping. Or maybe she's dead.

I try not to let the thoughts show on my face. I take another bite.

Above the sink, a window looks out to the backyard. I can see an old steel clothesline down near the back fence. On the left side of the yard is the back end of the garage, and behind that is a small tin shed.

Almost the whole yard is concrete, which is not like anything I've ever seen before. There's a patch of round grass in the middle, almost like they forgot to do that bit. Don sees me looking.

'Vince over the road helped me do the concrete. He's a lovely bloke. Italian fella.' He clears his throat. 'The missus was the one into gardening. She had roses and everything out there. Kept everything perfect.'

We go quiet again, and the clock gets even louder this time. I wonder if I should say or ask something about Mrs Don. Maybe something like they do in the drama shows Mum likes. Like they do on the telephone in *Sons and Daughters*.

'I'm sorry,' I say.

Don frowns. 'What's that?'

'I said I'm sorry.'

'About what?'

'About Mrs Don.'

He smiles.

'It was a while back, Jimmy. But thanks all the same.'

We go quiet again. I wonder if I should say something else, but I can't think what. The clock is doing all the talking.

I wonder why he got rid of the garden. Maybe he never liked it, or maybe he didn't like Mrs Don very much. I should've asked. We all look out the window, even Sam, like the answers might be out there.

After what feels like forever, Don stands up.

'We'd better get cracking, eh?'

•

We go into the garage through a side door, from the backyard. Inside, it's cool and dark and smells like grease. It takes a while for my eyes to adjust.

'This is where I spend most of my time,' Don says.

The garage is much bigger than I expected. Much bigger than it looked from outside. He flicks a switch, and two long fluoro lights hum and flicker to life. Along each wall is a dark timber bench, and the walls are hung with all sorts of tools.

In the middle, taking up most of the space, is a big black car. An old-fashioned one.

'Austin A40,' he says. 'The Devon. Don't see many nowadays. For good reason, I'd say.'

It looks a bit like one of those old taxis they use in England, and it's coated with dust. Don taps the roof.

'Long-term project. Even longer now my back's shot.'

'Looks good,' I say.

'From the outside, maybe. But there's a lot wrong under the hood. Suspension is rooted too. Good thing is, she's pretty easy to work on. When I can be arsed, that is. I'll have to keep the old Crown as my runabout for a while yet.'

He walks around the car to the garage door, leans down slowly, and pulls it up. Light floods inside, and the air suddenly smells much fresher.

'So here's the machine in question.'

The Firefox looks pretty sad sitting out on his driveway in front of the Crown, with the steering rope slung to one side. The tyres are still flat, and I notice now that the plastic seat is cracked. Maybe it was already like that, but maybe it was from when I sat in it. It looks even worse than when me and Danny took it out of the shed, especially next to the Austin.

Don circles it with a finger at his lips, studying every angle. 'Hmm,' he says, and he frowns like he's looking at a complex piece of machinery.

'It's a bit rough,' I say.

Don scratches his chin.

'She's got some charm, that's for sure. When's your race?'

'Two weeks.'

He nods. 'We'll have her shipshape by then.'

I should've told him about *Quiet Sam*. It was probably the right moment to say it, even better than the first time, but I feel like he'll be disappointed. He'd got us that cake and everything. Plus, Mrs Don is dead. I didn't know that before.

He crouches down slowly, picks up the cart, then carries it to the bench on the far wall. It's like a sick patient, and he's the doctor who is going to save it. He places it down, rubs his hands together.

'Now,' he says. 'Let's give her a proper look.'

•

Don spends most of the morning taking out the screws and bolts that hold *The Firefox* together. He says once we've got it all apart, we can work on each component separately.

'Always the best way,' he says.

First thing is to sand the wood and oil it, which we're gonna do in the afternoon. He's gonna show us how. Then we might regrease the axles and bearings, if there's time.

At lunchtime, he decides we should sit out in the backyard. He gets a fold-out table from the shed, and we carry the kitchen chairs outside.

'Nice to get a bit of sun,' he says.

He makes us a jug of lime cordial with ice cubes, and brings out three glasses. It's super sweet and delicious.

'I've got some sausage rolls coming in the oven. You like sausage rolls?'

'Yep,' I say.

'How about you, Sam?'

Sam looks at him.

'He likes them,' I say.

'Beauty. They're my favourite too. The missus used to make them from scratch, the pastry and everything. She'd even mince the meat herself. They were magnificent.' He shakes his head. 'Never had the patience, myself.'

I imagine Mrs Don from the photo on the mantlepiece, making the sausage rolls in her wedding dress with a meat mincer. Don is eating them in his wedding suit, being careful not to drip any sauce. They would have been delicious.

'I got some at the supermarket, so they won't be anywhere near as good,' he says. 'But if you're hungry, it'll do.'

He refills Sam's glass.

'Thanks for helping us with *The Firefox*,' I say.

'Pleasure, Jimmy. Always like being on the tools, just as long as the back holds up.'

'You've got a good garage.'

He shrugs. 'When I was a mechanic, I used to do a bit of work at home. Cash on the side, you know. For mates and such.' He takes a big drink. 'Your place doesn't have a garage, does it?'

I shake my head. 'Nah, just a little shed out back.'

Don nods. 'I've seen Mick's Pacer out on the front lawn there. Beaut car, that one.'

'Yeah. He loves it.'

'I bet. Tell him if he ever needs help with it, I'm happy to take a look. I've worked on heaps of Valiants. Hundreds. Thousands even.'

Don refills my glass, then his own. He has the back door open, and I can smell the sausage rolls cooking. It's making me hungry.

Don eyes me. 'When's he out?'

There's a ringing from inside, and he gets up before I can answer.

'Won't be a tick.'

Sam shifts in his seat.

'It's okay,' I say. 'We're gonna eat in a minute. We'll do a bit of work after, then go home.'

I'm starting to wonder if I'll get time to train with Danny and Chadwick. I know Danny will be really annoyed if I don't show.

Don comes back out with three big sausage rolls on a plate, and a bottle of tomato sauce. The sausage rolls smell great.

He puts the plate down on the table with a wave of his arm, like he's on *The Price Is Right*. Or like a waiter in a fancy restaurant. It's pretty funny.

'Lunch is served, gentlemen.'

•

It takes a long time to sand all the wooden bits. Much longer than I thought. Don showed us how with the sandpaper. You have to do it with the grain of the wood. He said if you go across the grain, it ruins it. Plus, I have to be careful around the letters. That takes extra long.

'Careful there,' Don says. 'That's Mick's handiwork, is it?'

'Yep.'

'Double the reason, then. Don't think he'd be too pleased if you took it off. When did you say he was getting out?'

'I'm not sure,' I say. Then I remember what Mum said, 'Depends if he gets parole.'

He nods. 'Fair enough.'

Don gives Sam a sanding block, and he helps him do the tricky bits. It's slow going, but Don says doing it slowly is the only way. He says to do things properly, you have to take your time.

'If you rush it, or use a belt sander, it strips everything away. It'd be quicker, but you'd lose the nice grain. You'd lose the patina, the imperfections, the character. It's better by hand. You get a better feel for things. Take your time, and do it right. That's the pleasure of it.'

It's nice in Don's garage, and nice listening to him talk about sanding. There's a cool breeze after lunch, so he closes the garage door halfway. It feels safe and secret inside.

Don has the radio on. It's people talking mostly, with interviews and things like that. I've never heard a radio station like it. They're talking about politics and science and books. It doesn't have any music, and there's news every hour. It's nice to listen to while we work, even if I don't understand most of what they talk about.

We don't get all the wood finished, though. We don't get to oil it. And we don't even start on the axles or the bearings.

'Next time,' Don says. 'Once we oil it, you'll see how nice it comes up. That's when you'll see the hard work was worth it.'

Don opens the garage door, and I know straight away. I can't believe the day has gone so quick. I've definitely missed out on training. Danny is gonna be furious.

Still, I'm pretty happy about the day we've had. And I think Sam really liked it too.

'Thanks for your help with everything,' I say.

Don shakes his head.

'You boys did most of it. And it was you and Mick who built the billycart in the first place. That's where the real work is.'

It's nice of him to say it.

'It's gonna come up a treat,' he says. 'You'll see. Good as new.'

I can't tell him about *Quiet Sam*. It's too late. He's so happy with the work we've done. He'll be too disappointed.

Plus, it'll be good to have *The Firefox* fixed for when Mick gets out of jail. He'll be pretty impressed.

'We can do a bit more after school this week, if you're keen. While we've got a bit of light.'

Sam takes my hand and gives it a squeeze.

'That'd be good,' I say.

Me and Sam walk down the driveway. Don follows, then opens the gate for us. As we step onto the footpath, light rain starts to fall.

Don looks up to the darkening sky. 'Looks like it might settle in. How about I give you boys a lift home?'

'In the Austin?' I say.

He laughs. 'Wouldn't get very far, Jimmy. We'll take the Crown.'

•

When we pull up out front, the rain is heavier. I can see the light on in the kitchen, and I wonder if Mum is cooking dinner. Even though lunch was more than we'd normally have to eat, I'm already really hungry.

'Thanks for the lift, Don,' I say.

'No worries, Jimmy.'

Don cuts the engine, then gets out to help Sam from the back seat.

'Might just say g'day to your mum.'

We walk quickly through the front yard, but I see Don glance at the Pacer.

'Good he's got it under cover,' he says. 'They can rust a bit.'

When we get to the front door, I can already smell something cooking. Maybe sausages. It gives me a good feeling.

'Mum,' I call out. 'Don's here!'

We go into the lounge room and Mum comes in from the kitchen. Her face is a bit red, almost like she's embarrassed to see Don. She smiles and wipes her hands on her apron.

'G'day, Don.'

'G'day, Nicki. Just thought I'd drop the boys home.'

It's always weird hearing people say Mum's name. Her proper name is Nicole, but no one calls her that.

'They've been hard at it, these two,' Don says.

I try not to smile, but I can't help it.

'Thanks, Don,' Mum says. 'Get you a beer?'

'Wouldn't say no.'

'Only got Carlton Light. That okay?'

'If it's wet and cold, I'm happy.'

Mum goes back out to the kitchen, and I turn on the telly. The news is on, which is always incredibly boring. Even worse than Mum's drama shows.

Mum comes back and passes a can to Don.

'Cheers,' he says.

'Take a seat?' Mum says.

'Nah, I'll knock this back quick.' He takes a deep swig. 'You've got to feed these boys, and I've got to get dinner on as well.'

Bob Hawke is being interviewed by someone, and we all look at the telly for a bit, but I don't think anyone is really watching.

'How's work been going?' Don says.

Mum shrugs. 'They've cut my hours.'

'Really?' He frowns. 'The bastards.'

She nods.

Don takes another deep swig of his beer.

'Well,' he says, 'if you're ever stuck, for bills and such, I'd be happy to help you out.'

Mum crosses her arms. 'Thanks, Don. That's good of you.'

He shakes his head. 'No worries at all. Promised your mum as much.'

The ads come on the telly, and it's the Razzamatazz one with the song you can never get out of your head. Just as it finishes, I hear a car pull up out front, then a door slam. The car beeps its horn.

'I'd better head off,' Don says.

I hear the front door open, then footsteps in the hallway.

My heart sinks. I didn't think he'd be back from shearing so soon. Part of me hoped he might never come back.

Charlie comes into the lounge room with a bag slung over his shoulder. When he sees Don, he goes all stiff.

'Well, well,' he says. 'Look who's here.'

'Charlie,' Don says.

Charlie eyes Mum, then Don. 'What brings you round?'

'Just giving the boys a lift home. Given the weather.'

'Is that right?'

I can tell it's the sort of question he doesn't really want an answer to. The sort adults ask when they don't like each other much. Like the way they talk on telly.

Don drinks the last of his beer, passes the can to Mum.

'Thanks, Nicki,' he says. 'I'd better run.'

Charlie smiles, but there's a mean look in his eyes.

'Yeah, you better run,' he says. 'That's one thing you're good at.'

Don stops, turns and looks at him for a second, then shakes his head.

Mum follows Don to the door, then goes outside. I can hear them talking for a minute out front, but I can't hear what they're saying. After a bit, I hear Don's car starting up.

Charlie gets himself a beer from the fridge, then sits on the couch next to Sam. The ads are over, and the news is back on. It must be nearly finished. I wonder if I should ask Charlie something about his shearing, but I'm not sure what. He stares at the telly, so I stare at it too.

Mum comes back inside. She stops in the lounge, right in front of the telly.

'You could be a bit nicer,' she says.

Charlie doesn't look at her. He looks through her legs at the newsreader, takes a swig of his beer.

'Why should I?'

'He's been good to the boys.'

Charlie shakes his head.

'He can go fuck himself.'

I wonder why Charlie is being so mean about Don, but I know I can't ask. Mum sighs and heads back to the kitchen. I'm still looking forward to the sausages, but not as much as before.

Charlie smiles and puts his arm around Sam, but I can tell Sam doesn't like it.

'It's good to be back,' he says.

SEVEN

We've been training every second night. Even so, Danny is making such a big deal about the day we missed.

'We have to make up for lost time,' he says.

It annoys me a bit. It feels like he's already blaming me in case we don't win. He doesn't know that I was trying to keep Don happy, and keep him happy too.

All the training means me and Sam aren't able to go back to Don's yet. When he dropped Sam off after school and asked if we were coming over, I told him we were busy.

'No worries,' he said. 'There's no rush from my end. When did you say the race was?'

'Week and a bit.'

'Plenty of time,' he said. 'Especially the rate you boys work at.'
I didn't tell him about the training with Danny and Chadwick.
I didn't tell him about *Quiet Sam*. I wasn't lying, not exactly.
I'll definitely tell him the next time we go round.

•

After school on Wednesday, a couple of grade six kids see us
training with *Quiet Sam* at the resi. Darren Finn and Jeremy
Mullens. They're two of the biggest kids in grade six, and they're
gonna be in the race too.

When they see us, they start chucking rocks. But there's no
way they can hit us through the trees. Chadwick reckons they
must be worried.

'They must think we're a real threat.'

If we beat them, they'll be pretty pissed off. They might
even try to bash us. Mullens bashed Danny once after school
for no reason, and it was pretty bad.

But it kind of makes us more determined. We do our best
training so far. Chadwick got his dad to lubricate the wheels and
axles on *Quiet Sam*. He did it after I told him about what Don
was planning to do with *The Firefox*. I didn't tell them about
the bearings, though, because I forgot. But even just doing the
wheels and axles made a really big difference.

Later on, after dinner, Mum asks about the race.

'How's it all going?' she says. 'You boys have been training
a lot.'

'Good. I think we've got a real chance.'

She smiles. 'Well, maybe I should come watch then.'

My chest felt full right up when she said that. Mum has never come watch me do anything sporty. It isn't her fault, though. It's because I'm not very good at sports, apart from rounders. And that isn't a real sport.

•

On Friday, Danny decides we'll have our last training session at the resi after school.

Even though it's Chadwick's cart, Danny's the one mostly in control of our training program. Chadwick is in charge of tactics, so I'm in charge of steering. It wasn't officially decided or anything, it's just the way it's worked out.

Danny reckons we should be 'tapering', which is something he saw on telly. Before a big race, athletes ease off their training so they're nice and fresh on the day.

'Rob de Castella does it,' he says. 'For the marathon.'

I'm not sure it's the real reason, though. It's probably because he's scared that Finn and Mullens will come back, but I don't say so. Especially not in front of Chadwick. I don't want to embarrass him.

After school, I pick up Sam from the bus stop and we head straight to the resi. He squeezes my hand really tight.

'It's just for a bit. It won't take long.'

'Okay,' he says.

'Things are looking good. It looks like we might win.'

'Yep.'

'Mum and Mick will be happy if we win, don't you think?'

He squeezes my hand again.

'Plus, if we fix *The Firefox* up, Mick will be extra happy.'

We walk for a bit without saying anything.

'Not long now till he gets out.'

'Okay.'

'That'll be good, won't it?'

'Yep.'

'Charlie won't hurt Mum again. Mick won't let him.'

'Yep.'

It makes me feel good when I say it. Even if Charlie has promised, and it's his last chance, having Mick around will be even better.

'You want to go to Don's again?'

'Okay.'

'Me too. We'll go tomorrow.'

When we get to the resi, Danny and Chadwick are already waiting. Danny is sitting on a tree stump, and he looks pretty pissed off.

'I had to wait for Sam,' I say. 'The bus was late.'

Chadwick points to the billycart.

'Check it out,' he says. 'We've made some improvements.'

I notice there's a piece of black velvet hanging from the back of the seat, a bit like a cape. It has gold lettering across the centre, cursive style.

Quiet Sam.

'Mum made it,' Chadwick says. 'Looks good, doesn't it?'

My chest feels full right up again. It was really nice of his mum. Nice of Chadwick too.

'Looks great,' I say. 'You see it, Sam?'

'Yep.'

'It's just for looks,' Danny says.

I can tell he's still pissed off, but I pretend I don't notice.

It was really nice of Mrs Chadwick to make it. I wish we could do something like that for *The Firefox*. I'd ask Mum, but I'm not sure she'd know how. I've never seen her do any sewing. Nan used to knit sometimes, but I think that's different.

•

We have another practice along the tracks, and there's no sign of Finn or Mullens.

'We should finish early,' Chadwick says. 'Save our energy.'

Danny agrees, because he reckons we should check out the carny camp on the other side of the resi.

'Won't take long,' he says.

The carnival comes every year at Easter time, and the carny folk always set up camp at the trotting track, near the resi.

But the carny itself is at Ryall Park, which is in the main part of town.

The carny is pretty good. Sam loves the dodgems, but I prefer the Cha-Cha, so we choose one or the other each year. The Cha-Cha is a ride with big steel arms attached to seats that spin around like crazy. It's great. The carny has a circus too, but I've never been. It's too expensive, and I'd much rather go on the rides.

Me and Sam go to the carny most years, but we missed out last year. Mum didn't have enough money, and it's no good going if you can't go on the rides.

'We should hide the billycart, though,' Danny says. 'In case Finn or Mullens come back.'

'Nah, there's no need,' Chadwick says.

Danny looks pretty annoyed. I think it's because Chadwick disagreed with him. He gets funny sometimes about things like that.

Even if Danny is in charge of training, and I'm in charge of steering, it seems like Chadwick definitely has the final say on things.

•

The carny folk have set up camp in a big circle with their trucks and caravans. On the near side, they've laid out their circus tent flat on the ground. A couple of scraggly looking blokes are checking it over. On the far side of the camp there's three trucks lined up end to end.

'The animals must be in those,' Chadwick says. 'For the circus.'

We walk further along the edge of the resi, to try to see around the other side of the trucks. And that's when we see it.

I've never seen an elephant in real life, apart from on the telly. He's huge and wrinkly, with a long trunk, big ears and sleepy eyes. He's really beautiful. He doesn't see us, I don't think, and he takes a couple of steps sideways.

There's hay on the ground all around him, and he doesn't have any tusks. He looks about a thousand years old.

'They didn't have one last year,' Chadwick says.

'They probably caught him in Africa,' Danny says.

Sam stares and squeezes my hand tight.

The elephant's back left leg has a big steel ring around the bottom of it, almost like a bracelet. It's joined to a chain that's driven into the ground with a long steel peg. He can't move very far.

I wonder if they ever let him loose, or take him out for walks. The carny folk probably don't have time for things like that. They probably just have him chained up all the time, apart from the circus show.

We stand there looking at him for ages, and no one says a word. It's something I don't think I'll ever forget.

•

When it's time to head home, me and Sam split up from Danny and Chadwick. We decide to go the long way. I take Sam's hand in mine.

'We'll go to the railway line,' I say. 'See if there's a train coming.'

Dusk is always the best time to see the trains. They usually only come through once or twice a day, and it's usually early or late. It's different on weekends, though.

It's nearly dark by the time we get there, and I can tell Sam is tired. We sit down and wait, but I wonder if we've already missed it.

But then, just as the sun is beginning to set, I can hear something. Sam does too, and he stands up.

'Don't get your hopes up,' I say. 'It might just be freight.'

But when it starts coming around the bend, I know straight away it isn't freight. The engine is bigger on those ones, and they're slower.

It's the *Southern Aurora*.

It has all its lights on, and it looks pretty incredible. All bright, shiny steel. It toots its horn as it gets near, and Sam covers his ears.

There aren't as many people in the carriages as other times, but we wave all the same. None of them wave back. It must be too dark for them to see.

'One day it'll be us on that train,' I say. 'On our way to Sydney. We'll wave to all the people in the towns along the way.'

Sam grips my hand tight.

'Or we'll go the other way to Melbourne. Me and you. Mum and Mick too.'

Sam starts humming. It's dark, and it's getting cold, but I'm really glad we came.

EIGHT

When we get home, Charlie is in the lounge room. He's sitting on the couch watching telly, drinking a can of Carlton Light. I get a sick feeling.

'G'day, boys,' he says.

'Where's Mum?' I say.

He taps the side of his head.

'She's got a headache. Gone to bed for a bit of a spell, so you'll need to keep the noise down.'

It's strange for Mum to get a headache. I hope she's okay. I hope nothing like Brownville has happened again. Things have mostly been better since then, but things can change really fast sometimes. Especially with the Kaiser around.

I see it sitting on the kitchen bench. I want to check it, but I don't want Charlie to see.

I shouldn't have gone the long way home. I shouldn't have gone to see the *Southern Aurora*. I should've come home and kept an eye on Mum.

Charlie pats the seat beside him.

'Sit down,' he says.

I don't really want to sit next to him, but it's hard to say no to grown-ups. Nearly impossible.

'*It's a Knockout*'s on,' he says.

'Okay.'

I sit beside him, and Sam sits on the floor. *It's a Knockout* is a pretty stupid show, with teams from different states in weird competitions pouring coloured liquid into measuring tubes. You can never get the music out of your head.

I'm hungry, and I know Sam will be too, but we'll have to wait for Mum. Apart from the barbecue at Brownville, I've never seen Charlie cook. I spose he must at his place, but I've never seen him do it.

When the ads come on, Charlie asks me to get him another beer. I see there's lamb chops in the fridge, on a plate with the Glad Wrap on. I hope like anything we're having those. Maybe Charlie brought the chops back from when he went shearing, from one of the sheep. I pull a can from the six pack and it's icy cold.

When I come back in, I catch Charlie flicking Sam on the side of the head. He stops when he sees me.

'Thanks, Jimmy,' he says.

Charlie cracks the can and takes a big swig.

'That hits the spot. How you boys been going?'

'Good.'

He nods. 'And your mum?'

I shrug. 'She's okay.'

He takes another swig, keeps his eyes on the telly. *It's a Knockout* is back on, but it's nearly at the end.

'Any blokes been around while I've been away?'

I look at Charlie, but he keeps watching the telly. There's a smile at the edge of his lips, but I don't think it's a real one.

'Nah,' I say. 'Only Don when he dropped us off the other day.'

'You sure?'

I nod. 'Yep.'

'Wouldn't be lying to me, would ya?'

I feel my face getting hot.

'Nah.'

He smiles, but it's more like a proper one this time.

'How about you, Sam? You seen anyone around?' He taps Sam on the top of the head. 'Is anyone home in there?'

Sam doesn't answer.

Charlie drains the rest of his can, then lets out a loud burp.

'Scuse me,' he says. 'By the way, your mum told me about the billycart race.'

'Yeah?'

'Yeah. Said you boys are nailing it. Reckons we should come watch.'

I really wish she hadn't told him. But I try not to show it, because I know that's what she'd want.

'We're going okay, but we're up against the grade sixes. So you don't have to come if you don't want to. If you're busy, I mean.'

He shrugs. 'We'll see.'

He crushes the empty can in his hand. I notice there's a scratch on his forearm and it's bleeding a bit. I wonder how he did it.

'Old Don been helping you much?'

'Yep.'

Charlie keeps staring at the telly, even though it's just the ads, so I stare at it too. I'm not really watching, though.

'Been behaving himself?'

I don't really know what he means.

'Yeah,' I say.

'That's good.' He clears his throat. 'Hasn't mentioned me, has he?'

I remember Don asking about Mum and Charlie ages ago, but I don't think that counts.

'Nah.'

Charlie nods. 'We go way back, me and Don.'

He stops looking at the telly, and he looks right at me instead.

'You can't ever trust that prick,' he says. 'So watch your back.'

I feel my face getting hot again, and I'm not sure what to say.

'You get my drift?'

'Yep,' I say, even though I don't.

I see something shift in his eyes, just for a split second. It's like he has another thought and is about to say it, but decides not to.

NINE

Next day, me and Sam are meant to go back to Don's. We're meant to oil the boards and grease the axles. We're meant to put *The Firefox* back together.

But Sam can't come.

'He's got something on at the school,' Mum says. 'It's the barbecue they do every year with the parents and staff.'

I remember the barbecue from last year. They had sausages and hamburgers, plus a clown who made animals out of balloons. The clown was okay.

'Do I have to come?' I say.

She shrugs. 'Not if you don't want to. Charlie's gonna drive us. He's gone to get the GT again.'

I'm disappointed Sam can't come with me. He'd really liked it last time. And I'm a bit disappointed I won't get another ride in the GT. But I don't want to let Don down. Plus, I need to get *The Firefox* ready for when Mick gets out. That's more important than the barbecue, or the GT.

Mum goes to the sink and turns on the tap. It makes the pipes clang for a second, but then it stops. She's got her long pyjama pants on, and the t-shirt she wears to bed. Both are wrinkled. I can see there's a bruise under the sleeve of her left arm. It's purple and red. It looks like someone grabbed her arm really tight. Someone with really strong hands.

'Is everything okay?'

As soon as I say the words, I wish I'd just stayed quiet.

She turns off the tap. 'What's that?'

I clear my throat and ask again. It sounds even worse the second time.

She stares at me for a second, frowns, then turns back to the sink.

'Of course, Jimmy. Why do you ask?'

I should say something about the questions Charlie was asking me, or something about her arm. Or maybe even something about how Charlie's mean to Sam, but I can't think of how to say it.

'It's nothing,' I say.

•

When I get to Don's, he's already got the garage door open. He's standing at the wooden bench, adjusting a spanner. It's a big one, like plumbers might use. He doesn't have his overalls on this time, just pants and a shirt. He looks a bit surprised to see me.

'Morning, Jimmy. Where's Sam?'

'He couldn't come.'

'Why's that?'

He leans over the bench and hangs the spanner on the wall. Everything has a place there.

'Had to go to his school barbecue. Mum's going too.'

He smiles and shakes his head. 'Ah yeah, that's right. That thing they do every year to try to keep the parents sweet.' He eyes me. 'Is everything okay?'

'Yeah.'

'You sure?'

'Yep.'

'Looks like there's something on your mind.'

I wish my face didn't show what I was feeling. I wish I could hide it better.

'Nah, I'm okay.'

He keeps looking until I look away.

'Righto then,' he says. 'Well, we'd better get stuck in seeing as we're a man down. We'll have morning tea when we're done with the sanding, as a reward.'

I thought we'd nearly finished the sanding last time, but it turns out there's a fair bit more to do. He gives me a finer grain of sandpaper this time, 180 grit, and it helps get the edges super smooth.

'Pays to start with a coarser grain, then a finer one,' he says. 'It's the last ten per cent that really counts with sanding. With everything, really.'

He has the radio on again, but this time it's music. It sounds like jazz, with trumpets and stuff, but I can't be sure. I prefer the talking station he had on last time, but I don't say so.

When we're done with the boards, Don dusts them off with a soft cloth.

'Beautiful,' he says. 'Time for smoko, I reckon. We'll have morning tea out back.'

This time, we don't have the Lions fruit cake. Instead, it's something he baked himself. It's still warm from the oven, and it smells incredible.

'Lemon cake,' he says. 'The missus used to make it. Still got the recipe on the fridge from the *Women's Weekly*.'

He places the cake on the table between us. It's round with a hole in the middle. He's made me a Milo and a tea for himself. The Milo is a bit too strong, but still nice. I wish Sam had come. He would've loved the cake.

Don raises his mug.

'Cheers,' he says, and we clink them together.

We both go quiet while we eat. The cake is soft and warm and really delicious. It's lemony, but without being sour. I remember what Charlie said, how I should watch my back. It doesn't make any sense.

But mostly, I just hope Mum's all right. Charlie must've hurt her arm, he must've squeezed it really tight. I really hope he doesn't hurt her again.

'It's really nice,' I say.

'Bit dry.'

'Nah,' I say. 'It's good.'

He shakes his head.

'Thanks, Jimmy. But it's nothing on hers.'

I decide to ask him about Mrs Don. It feels like the right time, like he wants me to.

'What happened to her?'

He blows on his tea, takes a sip. He looks out over the back-yard, then back at me.

'The missus?'

'Yeah.'

He sighs, takes another sip of his tea.

'Alzheimer's,' he says. 'You know what that is?'

I shake my head.

'Dreadful thing, Jimmy. The person you know just slowly starts to fade away. It's like a long, painful goodbye.'

He looks past me, to somewhere in the distance. His eyes have gone a bit glassy, almost like he might be about to cry, but he keeps it in. It's like he's remembering and feeling something painful all over again. I shouldn't have said anything.

'I kept her home as long as I could, but it got too hard to look after her. So she ended up at the nursing home.'

I wonder if I should tell him about Nan, that she was in the nursing home too. It might make him feel better. He finishes his tea in one big gulp.

'Killed me taking her there. Hardest thing I've ever done.'

We both go quiet again. It's too late to talk about Nan. It's like I've missed the moment.

I wish Sam had come. Even though he doesn't talk much, it feels different when he's here. It's better. Easier. But it's good he's with Mum too, and that they're with other people. I don't think Charlie will hurt her if other people can see. He must've squeezed her arm so tight for it to bruise like that, or maybe he punched her. One of those two.

'It's a shame you never got to meet her,' he says. 'She used to be friendly with your nan, you know?'

'Really?'

'Yeah. That's how I know your mum. From when she was a little tacker.'

'What was she like?'

'Your mum?'

'Yeah.'

'Bit of a handful, full of beans, but a bright spark. The missus used to give her biscuits and such. Spoil her rotten. Your Aunty Pam too.'

I try to imagine Mum and Aunty Pam as little kids, with Mrs Don in her wedding dress holding a tray of biscuits. Don is in his wedding suit. They all look pretty happy.

'The missus would have loved you boys too. She was a ripper.'

His voice cracks when he says the last bit. He takes a deep breath, swallows, and I wonder again if he's about to cry. I have to say something, something to change the subject. Just so he doesn't feel so sad.

'How long have you lived here?' I say.

He clears his throat.

'This place?'

'Yeah.'

He shakes his head. 'Jesus, fifty years? First and only place we bought. It was a weatherboard when we got it, but now this stuff.'

He reaches out behind him and knocks his knuckles against the wall. I thought it was brick, but suddenly realise it's different up close.

'Asbestos,' he says. 'Bloke came door-to-door and sold it to her while I was at work. Said we'd never need to paint again.' He shakes his head. 'It's good stuff, durable, but ugly as sin.'

I don't know what asbestos is, but I decide not to ask. It seems like everything I say, he makes it about Mrs Don.

'He was right about never painting, though. And she knew I hated painting more than anything.'

The silence comes back, much louder than before. I wish we were inside where at least there's the noise of the clock. The clock is better than nothing.

•

After morning tea, we oil the boards. The colour is so much richer than before, and the grain shows through. Most of the boards are different colours. Red and brown and yellow. I wish Sam was here to see it.

'You've got blackbutt, pine, and Tassie oak too,' Don says. 'The blackbutt and oak are both hardwoods, which makes them a bit more durable, but the pine is easier to work with.'

Next we start the wheels. First, he shows me how to change the tubes, which he'd bought especially, brand new. It's pretty nice of him.

'Most times, you can repair the tube,' Don says. 'But these are too far gone.'

'How much do I owe you?' I say.

'For what?'

'The tubes.'

He smiles. 'Don't worry, Jimmy. It's my treat.'

It's pretty easy getting the old tubes out, but much harder getting the new ones in. It takes ages.

While I do the tubes, he starts tightening the spokes on the other wheels. He says it'll make a difference to how it performs when cornering, and it'll help stop the wheels from buckling.

I never realised they were loose, or that you could tighten them. He even has a special tool for it, and he lets me do one.

'If the spokes are loose, she won't run true.'

Once I'm done, he shows me how to regrease the axle and the bearings. He shows me with the front two wheels, then I have to do the back ones. I undo the nuts, which were really stiff, then take the axle out. Then I fill it with grease, like he showed me.

While I work on the wheels, Don goes inside for a bit. While he's gone, I decide to have a closer look at the Austin A40. The Devon.

From the outside, it looks like something a bad guy might drive in a movie. Like a gangster in America. But inside, it looks really old fashioned, like something an old lady might drive.

When Don comes back, he catches me looking.

'You like it?' he says.

'It's really nice.'

'Bit of a beast. Not as nice as your brother's car, though.'

While I've been at Don's, I haven't been thinking much about Mick. I suddenly feel bad for it.

'I'll take you for a ride in it one day, once she's up and going.'

'Really?'

He nods. 'Sam can come too. But first things first. We've still got a fair bit of work to do on your machine.'

Even though there's still a lot to do, Don never seems to rush. He takes his time with everything. And he doesn't get frustrated or annoyed like Mick did when we were building the billycart.

I used to think you'd get less patient when you got old, because you've got less time left. But I wonder if the opposite might be true. With Don, anyway. And with Nan.

When I'm done with the wheels, Don squeezes my shoulder. 'That's damn fine work, Jimmy,' he says. 'Damn fine.'

·

This time, there's no sausage rolls for lunch, but we still sit outside. Don makes us a cheese and ham sandwich each.

'Sorry I haven't got anything hot, but I spent all morning on that bastard cake.'

He'd put relish with the ham, which I've never had before. It's sweet and salty all at once.

'It's really nice,' I say.

I hear a sprinkler come on next door. It must be one of those tall, revolving ones, because every twenty seconds or so, the water smacks against the fence. We're both quiet, and the sun is warm on my skin. It's good just sitting there like that, without talking or anything.

'Still hungry?' he says.

'Nah.'

I am a bit, but I don't want to be greedy.

'How's things at home?'

'Okay,' I say.

I wonder if he knows something. Something about what happened at Brownville. And the time before too. He couldn't know about the new bruise, though.

He crosses his arms.

'Charlie still coming round?'

'Yep.'

'How's he been?'

I shrug. 'Okay.'

He nods.

'What do you make of him?'

I don't know what to say. I've never been asked anything like that about Charlie, or anyone grown up. Next door, on the opposite side of the sprinkler house, a dog starts barking. It sounds like a little one, a Jack Russell or something.

'I don't like him,' I say.

My heart pounds hard in my chest, but I'm glad I said it.

Don takes a deep breath in and out. He wheezes a bit.

'Your mum okay?'

He must know about Brownville. That's why he's asking all the questions. Maybe he saw her after, saw her eye. Or Mrs Simpson told him.

Don unfolds his arms.

'I don't mean to be nosy, you know?'

'I know.'

'I only ask because I know she doesn't have it easy. And I don't like Charlie either. We know each other. From a long time ago.'

'Really?'

'Yeah. He's younger than me, of course. But he did a bit of work at the garage, as an apprentice. Before he took up shearing and the like.'

I knew they went way back, but I never knew Charlie worked with Don.

'He was good on the tools, good hands, but his attitude was the problem. Shocking temper. Plus, he had light fingers, so the boss let him go.'

I already know about his temper, but I wonder what Don means about his fingers. I don't feel like I can ask, though. I don't want to keep talking about Charlie, because I'm worried Don might ask more questions about Mum, or maybe even about the Kaiser. There's too much I have to keep hidden.

We both go quiet again.

'Thanks for the sandwich,' I say. 'And for helping with everything.'

'A pleasure, Jimmy. As long as my back holds up, I'm happy to help. And I'm happy for the company too.'

My face goes warm.

'It's been good having you around,' he says. 'Sam too. And I'm always here if either of you, or your mum, need me.'

I don't really know what to say to that.

'Okay,' I say. 'Um, I think *The Firefox* is gonna look really great.'

He smiles.

'I think you're right. It's a credit to you boys. You and Sam. You've done all the work. Mick too.'

I know it isn't completely true, but it's nice of him to say. I wish Sam could've heard it. Mick as well, even if he would've acted like he didn't care.

'When's the race again?' he says.

'This week coming.'

'Not much time for practice, then.'

I have to tell him. I don't want to hurt his feelings, but I can't keep pretending anymore. It doesn't feel right.

'I have to tell you something,' I say.

'Yeah?'

'Yeah. Well, it's just that we might not be using *The Firefox* after all.'

'No?'

My chest goes tight. I wish I hadn't said it. I wished I'd kept it a secret.

'I want to, but Danny wants to use Chadwick's one. So it's two against one.'

It isn't the complete truth, but not a total lie either. It's somewhere in between.

Don scratches his chin like he's thinking. The sprinkler next door stops. It's forever before he talks again.

'I'm glad you told me, Jimmy.'

'Yeah?'

'Yeah. It shows character.'

His voice is different, softer. Like he's hurt. I should've told him sooner, I should've told him the truth.

'Mum's gonna come watch,' I say.

'That's good,' he says.

I wonder if I should ask him to come too, but it feels too weird. I decide not to.

•

We don't quite finish putting it together, but almost.

The Firefox is looking pretty good. Not as flash as *Quiet Sam*, but there's something even better about it. Something more real, if that makes sense. Maybe it's because we did it ourselves. Mick too, even if he wasn't there.

'Only the seat and the rope to go,' Don says. 'Next time.'

We definitely could've finished it, though. There was time before it got dark. But I'm happy to come back again, because then Sam can come too.

'Maybe next weekend,' he says. 'I've got a few appointments these next couple of weeks, so I'll be busy. Johnny Burton will be driving Sam's bus during the week. Make sure to tell your mum.'

'Okay.'

'But we'll definitely have her done next time. You can take her for a spin, you and Sam.'

He lifts the garage door to let me out.

'Thanks, Don.'

He nods. 'A pleasure. And thanks for listening. About the missus, I mean. I know it got a bit heavy.'

We step out into the street. It's cooler than inside the garage, and I can smell cut grass in the air. Don follows me down the driveway to the front gate.

'One more thing,' he says.

'Yep?'

'There's something the missus used to say when things got me down, when the cards didn't fall my way. Something you might want to keep in mind.'

'Okay.'

'She'd say you only really see someone's character when the going's rough, when things are at their worst.'

He shuts the gate behind me.

'You're a good boy, Jimmy. Just try to remember that.'

TEN

On Sunday, Mum makes us pancakes for breakfast, and they're delicious. I put honey on mine, but Sam has his plain.

Mum is in her pink dressing gown and slippers, and she looks warm in the morning sun. She smells nice too. Not like the Kaiser, more like bed.

Charlie stayed the night, but he left early. I heard him talking with a man outside when I was still in bed. I heard a car horn, then a boot slamming shut. Charlie laughed at something the man said, but I couldn't hear what.

Me and Sam watched cartoons while we ate, with the plates on our lap. The Sunday cartoons are never as good, but they're okay. They're just the leftovers, the ones that aren't good enough to show on Saturday.

Mum sits on the armrest of the couch. She lights a smoke. She's watching the cartoons too, but not really. I don't know why grown-ups don't watch cartoons. I definitely will when I'm older.

When the ads come on, she says, 'You boys see the carny's in town?'

'Yeah,' I say. 'We saw their camp. They've got an elephant this year.'

'Yeah?'

'Yep.'

She takes a long drag, blows the smoke up toward the ceiling.

'You want to go? I can give you some cash. Might not be enough for the elephant, but you never know.'

'Really?' I say. 'Only if you've got enough.'

She taps her cigarette in the ashtray.

'Charlie gave me some,' she says.

It turns out Charlie has gone to another shearing job, with his mate who owns the GT. She says it's good because we'll have some extra money when he gets back.

'Keep the wolves from the door.'

But it's mostly good because he won't be around for a bit. She has her dressing gown on, but I know what's underneath. I know about the bruise and the strong hands.

She says the Kingswood still isn't running, so he's hoping to get enough cash from this job to fix it. He mustn't have learned enough about cars when he was working with Don to fix it himself.

'Just the three of us for a bit,' she says.

I'm glad, but I don't say so. I've been thinking about what Don said about Charlie, and I'm wondering if I should tell her. About the light fingers, about his temper. She already knows about his temper, though.

She gets up and cooks another pancake. She slides it onto my plate, even though I'm already full.

'Thanks, Mum.'

It's the last one, which is always the most delicious because it soaks up the butter from all the ones before. It's my favourite, and it's nice she gave it to me. I eat it slowly, so I can taste it more.

The Archie Show comes on, which is always pretty average. Mum lights another smoke.

'I got a phone call from your brother,' she says.

I put my plate down.

'Yeah?'

'Yeah.'

She bends down and takes Sam's plate. He looks a bit annoyed, even though he's finished.

'Guess what?' she says.

'What?'

'He got parole.'

She has a big smile, like I haven't seen in ages.

'Really?'

'Yep. He should be home in a couple of weeks. Once they sort the paperwork. But I'm not telling anyone yet, just in case something goes wrong.'

I wonder if she means something going wrong with the paperwork, or going wrong with Mick, or maybe even Charlie. Either way, I'm not going to tell Charlie about it.

'That's great,' I say. 'Hear that, Sam? Mick's coming home.'

Mum puts Sam's plate in the sink, turns on the tap. Sam keeps staring at the telly. *The Archie Show* is nearly finished, and *Get Smart* is on next. Sam really loves the beginning bit, with the doors opening and closing.

I'm happy Mick is getting out, but a bit worried too. It's been so long since I've seen him. I wonder if he'll be different this time. If he'll be better or worse, or maybe just the same. I wonder if he'll get in trouble again.

Mick was in trouble from when he was young. That's what Mum says. So the police have always picked on him. That's why he ended up in jail again. Most of what he did was small stuff. But when they added it all up, it looked bad.

That's what the police did. They added it all up to make it look really bad. The judge too. Especially the bit about when he bashed Keith. That's the main reason he got put in adult jail this time, I think. That's the main reason, but it wasn't the only one.

The other reason was because of the programs. I only know about it because I heard Mum talking with Charlie. She said the judge wanted Mick to deal with his addiction, and the best way was through the programs they have in adult jail.

Up till then, I never knew Mick took drugs. He'd never said anything about it, and I never saw anything. I guess that's the way he wanted it.

The phone rings in the hallway, and Mum goes to it.

I try to hear what she's saying, but it's hard with the telly. Sam cracks it if you turn it down.

When the ads come on, she says, 'Worth thinking about.' Then when the first ad ends, 'Can they hold the spot?' The last thing I hear her say is, 'I'll let you know.'

Then *Get Smart* comes on, and I can't hear the rest.

She comes back into the lounge room, lights another smoke, then stares at the telly.

'Who was it?' I say.

'Aunty Pam.'

Maxwell Smart and 99 are driving somewhere, but it looks really fake. Like they just have a screen behind them.

Mum takes a deep drag, holds it in.

'She's got a job in Fernvale for me,' she says. 'The supermarket she works at. In the deli.'

There's another lot of ads and Sam starts humming.

'That sounds good,' I say.

Mum looks at me, and the smoke wafts all around her. Even in her dressing gown, she still looks a bit like a movie star.

'I told her I'd think about it. Maybe once Mick finishes his parole.' She takes another drag of her smoke. 'We'd have to move there, but she thinks a fresh start might be good.'

Fernvale. A fresh start. A job in the deli.

It all sounds pretty great.

ELEVEN

Mum gave us twenty bucks for the carny, which is the most ever. She folded it between her fingers and passed it to me in a handshake, like it was a secret. It was pretty cool. She told me to be careful and not to lose it.

'Actually, I might come along for a bit,' she said. 'Just for the walk. I promise I won't cramp your style.'

We go down Manningham Street, which is the nicer way to Ryall Park, even though it takes longer. Manningham Street is where some of the biggest houses in town are, almost as big as Chadwick's, and it has green nature strips with big old trees in the middle.

The sun is warm, but it isn't too hot. It's nice to have the money, but even nicer that Mum has come with us. I wonder if we might see Danny at the carnival, or maybe Chadwick. I hope so.

'We might go on the dodgems first,' I say. 'Then get a dagwood dog for lunch.'

Sam starts humming.

I look at Mum. 'You know what a dagwood dog is?'

She smiles. 'You tell me.'

'It's like a hotdog on a stick, but it's deep fried. And you can only ever get them at the carnival.'

'Sounds great.'

Mum's wearing her black jeans and her blue flannel shirt for the first time since Brownville. The shirt covers her arms. She has her Le Specs on, and I can't see her eyes. The sun makes her hair look shiny, like someone from one of her drama shows on telly. Like *Dynasty*, but even better.

'We might have a go at the shooting range too,' I say.

The shooting range is pretty good, but also totally rigged. The sights are all out of line, and no one ever wins anything.

'They might have some new rides this year,' Mum says.

I know it will probably be the Cha-Cha and dodgems like every year, but I don't say so. At least this time, with twenty bucks, we'll be able to do both.

Even though I'm excited about the carny, I'm still thinking about Aunty Pam and Fernvale. I've never been to Fernvale, because it's a long way away, but I always thought it sounded pretty nice. It even got mentioned on the news sometimes, in the weather forecast, so I know it has to be pretty good.

It'd be good to move to a new place. A bit scary, but good. And it would definitely be better for Mum to have a new job.

I'd miss Danny, though. Probably Chadwick too. Maybe Don as well.

Still, in Fernvale, we could be like new people. No one in Fernvale will know about Mick going to jail. No one will know about Mum and the Kaiser. And we wouldn't live in Celestial Avenue anymore. Maybe they'd have a good school for Sam. Danny and Chadwick could always come visit. And we'd be far away from Charlie, far enough away that he couldn't hurt Mum. That's the most important bit.

The more I think about it, the better it sounds.

We're nearly at the carny when we see him. He's over the other side of the street, carrying some shopping. It's Mum who spots him first.

'There's Don,' she says.

She waves and calls out, and he crosses the street to meet us. He walks slow, like he's tired from carrying the bags. His face is all sweaty.

'G'day, Nicki.' Don eyes me and Sam. 'Where you all off to?'

'The carny,' I say.

He smiles. 'Good stuff. Great day for it, too.'

'Yep.'

Him and Mum start talking about boring things, like the weather and stuff. I'm pretty keen to get moving, but Mum seems happy to stay and talk to him. I wonder if she remembers him and Mrs Don from when she was little. Maybe she remembers the biscuits Mrs Don gave her and Aunty Pam. I decide I'll ask her later.

'Thanks again for helping the boys. With the billycart and everything,' she says.

Don shakes his head. 'It's been a pleasure. They've both got real aptitude, and they're not afraid of hard work. That's the main thing.'

I don't know what aptitude is, but it sounds like it's good to have.

'The boys tell you I'll be away for a bit?'

I'd forgotten to tell Mum about Don's appointments. About Johnny Burton and the bus.

'Everything okay?' she says.

'Yeah, yeah. Just some check-ups and whatnot. No good getting old, you know. But how are you going?'

There's something in the way he looks at Mum that's different when he says the last bit. Like he's serious, but a bit nervous about what she might say.

She shrugs. 'Could always be better.'

Don puts his bags down. I see he's got pork chops and potatoes in one, eggs and bananas in the other.

'How's Charlie been going?' he says.

'Good. Just gone off on a shearing job.'

Don frowns, like he's thinking.

'He's been treating you okay?'

I hold my breath.

She nods. 'Pretty good.'

Don looks at her, then his shopping bags, then her again.

'You sure?'

Mum swallows. 'Yep.'

Don takes a deep breath in and out. He sounds a bit wheezy.

'Well, just let me know if you need help with anything. I'm always around if you need me.'

'Yep. Thanks, Don.'

He clears his throat, looks up the street, then back at Mum.

'You shouldn't put up with any rubbish, you know? You don't deserve it. For the boys' sake too.'

It's hard to be sure of exactly what Don means, but I think I know. He's talking in a kind of secret code, like grown-ups do sometimes. Mum's speaking in the code too.

'I know,' she says. 'Thanks, Don.'

It's when they talk about something without really saying it, when they don't want to say the words. The meaning is underneath, and it's just too hard to say.

Even so, I'm glad Don said it.

•

They don't have any different rides at the carny. It's all much the same as the last time. The only new thing is a game where you have to scoop wooden fish out of the water, and you can win a prize. It's pretty random, though. There's no skill to it.

Sam has a go, but doesn't win anything. Then the carny bloke, who has dark skin and earrings in both ears, gives him another try for nothing.

When he doesn't get anything again, the carny gives him a stuffed toy anyway. A blue unicorn. It's pretty nice of him.

'Thanks,' I say.

The carny bloke smiles.

'No worries. He reminds me of my cousin.'

There's a long queue for the dodgems, so we go on the Cha-Cha first. Even though I like the Cha-Cha, it always freaks me out a bit, because it feels like you're gonna fly out of your seat.

I worry about the carny folk putting it together. I wonder if they tighten all the bolts and screws, and if anyone checks it afterwards. I doubt it.

They always have music playing during the Cha-Cha. You get to stay on for three songs. For our ride, it's 'Walk of Life', 'Jessie's Girl', and then 'The Final Countdown'.

Sam is as cool as a cucumber through the whole thing. He just sits there relaxed, like he's sitting at home on the couch. He sits on the left side, like always.

It's still a long wait for the dodgems, so we decide to queue up.

'It's good Mick's coming back, isn't it?' I say.

'Yep.'

'We might even go to the drive-in again.'

'Okay.'

I remember the time we went to the drive-in as clear as anything. Mick took me, Mum and Sam. And he paid for everything. Sam sat in the back and I was in the boot, so I'd get in for free. It was scary and dark in there, but exciting too.

Once we were in, we saw the end of *The Karate Kid*, which was the early movie, and then we watched *Indiana Jones and the Temple of Doom*, which was the movie Mick really wanted to see. *Indiana Jones* was pretty great, and the action scenes were incredible.

We ate hamburgers and drank Coke from little glass bottles, which they don't sell at the milk bar. It was a really good night, but I couldn't stay awake till the end. I'd be able to now, though. Easy.

After the dodgems, I see a couple of kids from school. David Knight is with his mum, but he doesn't say hello or anything, even though he looked right at me. He isn't really my friend, though. To be honest, none of the kids at school are my friends. Apart from Danny and Chadwick. Mainly Danny.

If we move to Fernvale, it isn't like I'm leaving heaps of friends behind. I might make some new ones too. And we'll get away from Charlie, so Mum won't have to put up with any rubbish, just like Don said.

David Knight's mum looks a bit like Jacki MacDonald from *Hey Hey It's Saturday*, but even skinnier. She sees me and Sam and gives me a look. I've seen that look from grown-ups heaps of times, so I know exactly what it means.

I don't want people to feel sorry for us. It's only because of bad luck that we live on the Avenue. And it's bad luck the police picked on Mick. It's bad luck too that we don't have much money, and that Charlie hurts Mum sometimes.

But all that's about to change.

TWELVE

It's the day of the race. Even though we've been looking forward to it, planning and training for ages, it feels like it came up really quick.

Before class, Mr Battista comes up to me and Danny. He says he's heard we've been training.

'I hope you boys win,' he says. 'But don't tell the grade sixes I said that.'

There's an announcement over the PA that there'll be no classes after lunch, so everyone is in a good mood. Even the kids who aren't in the race. Even some of the teachers.

Most of the other racers have brought their billycarts to school in the morning and put them in the shelter shed. But we decided not to. Chadwick thought it was better to take everyone by surprise.

At recess, we check out the other entries. None of them look as good as *Quiet Sam*. There's a couple of decent ones though, made out of steel. One is long and shaped like a rocket. It's Finn and Mullens' one. It's called *The Super Rocket*, which isn't very imaginative. We don't know who they have as a driver.

The weather is pretty cool, which is good. In training, when it was hot, Chadwick and Danny struggled a bit, so it feels like things are going our way. Chadwick says next year we'll start training a couple of months earlier, to make sure our fitness is better.

I haven't told him or Danny about Fernvale, because I'm not sure it's gonna happen. Plus, I don't want them to be distracted.

Even if Chadwick is a bit worried about our fitness, he's still pretty confident. So's Danny. They both reckon *The Super Rocket* will be fast in a straight line, but it won't be very agile on the corners, which is what Mr Battista said was most important.

I can hardly concentrate in class. Mr McGregor is teaching us about the old colonial times, and he says that people lived in dirt floor huts and life was pretty hard. He says most people couldn't read and they learned to play music to entertain each other. It all sounds pretty awful.

When the bell goes for lunch, my heart is fully pounding. Chadwick has paid for me and Danny to have a lunch order from the canteen, because he says we'll need the energy.

Chadwick's mum is meant to come before the end of lunchtime with *Quiet Sam*. We're sposed to meet her at the gate near the bike shed. She's sposed to come with Mr Chadwick, so he can help.

But when the bell goes, she isn't there.

Danny starts getting edgy. 'Where is she?'

'She'll be here,' Chadwick says. But I can tell he's a bit worried too.

Everyone is gathering around the course, and the first heat is already setting up at the starting line.

'What happens if we miss our heat?' I say.

Danny shakes his head. 'We're stuffed.'

Chadwick leans over the fence and looks up the street.

'Here she comes.'

When she pulls up in her station wagon, she looks pretty stressed. Her face is sweaty, and her hair's messed up. I've never seen her like that before. She winds down her window.

'What happened?' Chadwick says.

'I had trouble loading it up.'

She pops open the back, and me and Danny carefully lift *Quiet Sam* out onto the footpath.

'Didn't Dad help?' Chadwick says.

She doesn't answer.

'Are you staying to watch?'

She shakes her head.

'I'm sorry, Luke.'

She forces a smile. I can tell she's pretending, because I've seen my mum do the same one.

'Good luck, boys,' she says.

•

We kill it in our heat. The whole school is watching, and we lap all the other racers, except for the one in second place.

Chadwick and Danny make *Quiet Sam* fly like never before. All that practice on rough tracks in the resi makes the oval seem like nothing. It's so smooth and easy on the grass, and I love the feel of the air rushing past. It's incredible.

Mr Battista announces the results and times with a megaphone, and it's almost like we're famous.

'*Quiet Sam* looks like the one to beat!' he says.

In the final for our year level, it's a bit closer, but we still win easy enough. To be fair, none of the other carts are as good as ours. Though I reckon we might have won even with *The Firefox*. The other kids don't seem as organised as us, like they haven't prepared or trained properly.

In the final, we're up against *The Super Rocket*, which we expected, and *Blue Thunder* from grade four, which is a really nice-looking cart painted bright blue. It even has a rear spoiler.

There's a strange feeling in my chest I've never felt before. I imagine telling Sam and Mum that we won. Don too. I know they'll all be really happy. But most of all, I can't wait to tell Mick.

I know he'll be impressed, especially with the trophy and everything. It'll be the first trophy anyone in our family has ever won, I think.

Mr Battista reads out the teams and the name of each team member in the final. He does it all dramatic, like a boxing announcer on TV. It's great, especially when our names get read out. I try not to smile, to act cool, but I can't help it.

And then I see her. It's Mum. I'm so happy she came.

I wave, but she doesn't see me. She's smoking and standing away from the rest of the parents. I feel bad for her, because she's on her own, but I'm glad Charlie isn't there.

Suddenly, there's a loud bang.

I didn't realise Mr Battista was going to use a gun for the final, and it scares the crap out of me. Everyone runs for their carts.

'Quick!' Chadwick says.

I climb in and Danny and Chadwick start pushing. I can feel them pushing, but we aren't going anywhere. The crowd is yelling and clapping, and Danny and Chadwick are yelling too. Something is wrong with *Quiet Sam*. We're stuck on the starting line, not moving.

I watch as *The Super Rocket* goes around the first corner in the lead, and the grade fours are already thirty metres ahead of us.

Then Chadwick reaches over my shoulder and turns the steering wheel. That was the problem. I had the steering wheel locked left, so we couldn't go anywhere.

Once we get going, *Quiet Sam* flies like never before. We pass *Blue Thunder*, and soon enough we're over the ramp and on the last lap with *The Super Rocket*.

We're definitely faster than them, and gaining ground all the time. The crowd is cheering like mad.

With just one more lap, I reckon we would have caught them for sure.

•

Mr Battista looks disappointed when he announces the results. I reckon he really wanted us to win.

I feel sick. It was my fault.

'I'm sorry,' I say.

Chadwick doesn't say anything.

I look at Danny, hoping he might say something. It was my fault, I know it, but I didn't mean for it to happen. It was an accident.

Chadwick might not understand, but I know Danny will.

Eventually, he looks at me. And I see something I've never seen before. Something cold in his eyes.

'Danny?' I say.

He looks away.

THIRTEEN

The day after the race, me and Danny have Mr McGregor's class in the morning. Danny's sitting next to Ben Harvill, who normally sits next to Richard Bailey, but Bailey must be sick. Me and Danny normally sit together, so I figure he's still annoyed about the race.

I sit up the front next to Denis Anderson. Denis used to sit next to Michael Kreuse, but Kreuse's family have moved town, because his dad was a bank manager and got a job somewhere else.

Denis is one of the sporty kids, always with the latest gear. He doesn't look very happy when I sit next to him, but he doesn't say anything.

We do a writing exercise in the class, which Mr McGregor said we have to finish before we can go to recess. I'm a bit slower than most, but I get it done a few minutes after the bell.

Outside, when I look for Danny, I can't find him at our usual spot. We usually go to the monkey bars first, meet Chadwick, then decide what we're doing. Recess is only short, even shorter when McGregor holds you back, so you have to be quick to decide.

I look around the oval, thinking they might be playing cricket. But they aren't there either.

I spend nearly all of recess looking for them, which annoys me a bit. It's only right near the end that I spot them, sitting on a bench near the shelter shed.

When I get close, I see they're playing cards. UNO. It must be Chadwick's pack, because I know Danny doesn't have it.

'Can I play?' I say.

Chadwick puts down a Draw Four.

'Jesus! Again?' Danny says.

'Can I play next game?' I say.

Chadwick looks at me, then Danny, but doesn't answer. Danny keeps his eyes on his cards. It's like he's pretending I'm not there.

I stand there for a bit, wondering what to do. I know the bell will go soon, and recess will be over. I need to go to the toilet something fierce, but I decide to wait till the music starts over the PA. It gives you a warning before the bell goes.

'Who's winning?' I say.

Danny looks at Chadwick.

'You hear something?'

Chadwick looks at him but doesn't answer. Then he looks down at his cards.

There's a strange, twisting feeling in my chest. It hurts. I feel like crying, but I feel like punching Danny too. Punching him for being so unfair. I'll punch Chadwick too after I've punched Danny. I'll punch Chadwick for ruining everything.

The music starts playing on the PA. It's 'Walking on Sunshine', which they've been playing all year. Chadwick packs up the cards, puts them back in their box.

Danny stands up.

'Why are you being like this?' I say. 'It wasn't my fault.'

He doesn't answer straight away. It's probably just a few seconds, but it feels like much longer. The chorus is playing in 'Walking on Sunshine', and some of the kids walking past are singing along to it.

He speaks softly, so I barely even hear him over the music. But I definitely hear what he said. It's something he's never said to me before, and something I don't think I'll ever forget.

'You're such a loser, Jimmy.'

He looked me right in the eye when he said it.

•

It's hard being on your own at school, even just for a short time.

You feel like everyone is watching, and everyone knows you've got no friends. When you're with someone, you're more invisible. It's better like that.

I can't find them at lunchtime. They aren't at the monkey bars, or the shelter shed. I decide they must be hiding. I look around for a bit, then give up.

Mr Battista is on yard duty with two of the grade three kids. The kids are picking up rubbish, and Mr Battista is carrying the bin for them, which none of the other teachers ever do. I follow the three of them around for a bit. Mr Battista is wearing his Oakley sunglasses, the mirror ones with the fluoro trim, which are really flash and expensive. I stay quiet so he won't notice me.

After a bit, he turns around. I can't see his eyes with his Oakleys, but I know he's looking right at me.

'Everything okay?' he says.

'Yep.'

He tells off the grade threes for missing some rubbish, but smiles when he does it. I don't think I've ever seen Mr Battista get cross, even when kids are doing the wrong thing.

The sun is reflecting off his sunglasses, and he looks cool. Like he could be in a movie.

'You were unlucky yesterday,' he says.

Everyone must be talking about it, even the teachers. Everyone knows I'm a loser, like Danny said.

'Yep,' I say.

'Try not to stress,' he says. 'You'll have a good shot next year. You'll be favourites, I reckon.'

I shrug. 'Maybe.'

'Where's your mates?'

I feel the twisting in my chest again. Then my throat starts to hurt, which always happens before I cry.

'Dunno,' I say.

My eyes start to sting, but I blink and keep the tears inside.

Mr Battista takes off his sunglasses, folds them into the collar of his t-shirt.

'Listen, Jimmy. Sometimes, it's just that three's a crowd. Don't worry, they'll get over it.'

The sun goes behind a cloud, and it suddenly feels much cooler.

'Try not to worry about things so much.' He squeezes my shoulder. 'You can only do your best.'

'Yep.'

He sighs.

'I'll tell you something. But I want you to listen, okay?'

He crouches down, looks me right in the eye.

'It might not seem like it now, but the world is a bigger place than this school. Even this town. You understand?'

'Yep.'

'Things will get better, but you'll just have to trust me on that.'

I don't know how he can be so sure. Still, it's nice of him to say it.

•

Mrs Bon has seen me, but she doesn't say anything. She pretends I'm not there.

In the library, I get to be invisible and visible all at once, which is the best way sometimes.

I only have time to read a few pages of Tintin before the bell goes. It's *Tintin in America*, which I've read a few times, and it's still one of my favourites.

I try hard not to think about Danny and Chadwick, and what they're doing. Tintin helps, but not completely.

'You can only do your best.'

That's what Mr Battista said. I spose he's right, but it doesn't change how I feel.

On the way back to class, I do the thing he said. I do my best not to worry. Especially when I see Danny and Chadwick together, especially then. I do my best, like he said. But even then, it's hard not to cry.

PART THREE

ONE

It's just four days till Sunday. And on Sunday, Mick is gonna get out.

Charlie's been back from shearing for more than a week now, but Mum still hasn't told him about Mick coming home. I thought he might have his Kingswood running again, so I asked Mum if she could borrow it, but she didn't really answer.

Charlie's been acting all weird since he got back, and the Kaiser hasn't helped. They've been arguing a fair bit, mostly on the phone, so he hasn't been around as much as before. Not even for fish and chips on Friday.

I remember the last time Mick got out of jail. Me and Mum went to pick him up. Mum borrowed Aunty Pam's Ford Escort, and Aunty Pam stayed home and looked after Sam.

It was only the second time I've ever been to Sydney, but I didn't get to see the city or anything. Not up close. I could see the skyscrapers in the distance, but Mum said the smog was pretty bad.

'There's only one good thing to come out of Sydney,' she said. 'The highway.'

We went straight to the jail, which was in the middle of a big park. It had high walls and razor wire just like a normal jail, but it was called a Training School because it's only meant for young people. Still, it looked just like a jail to me. Just like one you'd see on TV. It looked nothing like any school I'd ever seen.

I had to wait for ages in the car. Mum went into reception to do the paperwork and all that, and it took forever. It was incredibly boring. She didn't leave the radio on because she was worried it'd flatten the battery.

It was taking so long that I wondered if maybe they were keeping Mick in for longer, or if Mum had made a mistake about the day.

When they finally came out, Mick was walking beside Mum, with his big duffle bag slung across his shoulders.

He looked different than the last time I'd seen him, even though it'd been less than a year. His hair was cut really short, and he was skinnier than before, but he looked better. It was like his eyes were brighter.

He smiled when he saw me, even though he was trying not to. Mum opened the boot and he chucked the duffle bag inside.

When he got in, he leaned into the back seat and punched me on the arm, but not hard.

'Dickhead,' he said, but he smiled when he said it.

'Get stuffed,' I said.

I could tell he was happy to see me.

•

Things were pretty good when Mick got out that time. The day he got out, we went out for dinner to celebrate. Mum had just started seeing Charlie back then, but he didn't come, even though Mum asked him to. He said it was a 'family thing', but I'm not sure that was the real reason.

We went to the pub and sat in the bistro, which is the special room out back. Mick told Mum not to make a fuss, but Mum said it was nicer than sitting in the bar. It had wooden panels on the walls and pictures of racehorses finishing their races, and there were other families there too. I even saw Ben Harvill with his parents. They didn't say hello, even though they saw us, but I didn't care that much.

I had a bowl of chips, and so did Sam. The chips were crinkle-cut, which are the most crunchy there is. I got gravy on mine, which I'd never had before. It was salty and delicious. It was Mick who suggested the gravy, and I wondered if he'd had it inside. I didn't ask. The only problem with the gravy was the chips went soggy before long, so you had to eat them quick.

Mick had a T-bone steak with pepper sauce and Mum had honeyed prawns. The honeyed prawns looked amazing. They were all battered and glistening with honey sauce dripped over them. Mum gave me one and it was just about the best thing I'd ever eaten. It was hot, crunchy and sweet all at once.

Mick ate every last bit of meat on his T-bone. He even picked up the bone and chewed on it, like he was Fred Flintstone. Sam really liked it when he did that. Mick said it was the best thing he'd eaten in ages.

Mum got us a jug of raspberry lemonade and a jug of Coke, which Mick said was a bit overboard, but we still managed to drink the lot. She had a glass of Moselle, which is like a fancy version of the Kaiser, and she only had one.

It was a great night. One of the best ever. Mick and Mum didn't argue even once. At the end, Mum said we should do it more often, not just on special occasions.

We didn't go again, though. And then, not long after, Mick went back to jail.

•

When I wake up on Sunday morning, I can hear Mum in the hallway. She's talking on the phone, but trying to be quiet about it. Sam is still asleep, so I stay in bed and try to listen.

'No,' she says. 'Jesus Christ, how many times do I have to tell you?'

I wonder who she's talking to. Maybe it's Charlie, and she's asking him to drop off the Kingswood. I hope he doesn't come with us to Sydney. I hope like anything it's just me, Mum and Sam.

'He's got nothing to do with it. Look, I don't want to go over it all again.'

She's still trying to be quiet, but I can hear her pretty clear. It takes ages before she talks again.

'Don't threaten me like that.'

Sam takes a deep breath in and out, then rolls over. I think he's about to wake up.

'I'm not listening to this.'

I hear the click as she puts down the phone. She sighs, then a few seconds later there's footsteps down the hallway.

I get out of bed slowly. Sam is still asleep, so I try to be as quiet as I can.

I go out to the kitchen. Mum is in her dressing gown, sitting at the table. She wipes her eyes with a tissue. Her hands are shaking.

'Is everything okay?' I say.

'Yes, Jimmy. Everything's fine.'

'Is Charlie coming?'

She shakes her head.

'No, he isn't.'

I'm glad he isn't coming over, but worried about how Mick will get home.

Mum wipes her eyes again, but the tears have mostly stopped.

'Did you ask him if we could borrow it? The Kingswood?'

'No, I didn't.'

I imagine Mick waiting for us up in Sydney at the jail with his duffle bag. I know he'll be disappointed.

'How come?' I say.

She lights a cigarette, takes a big breath, then blows the smoke up toward the ceiling. Her hands are still shaking.

'I told him we're finished, Jimmy. Me and Charlie.' She takes another drag, holds it in for longer. 'He doesn't treat us right.'

I'm not sure what to say. I wonder if it's because of what Don told her, how she shouldn't put up with any rubbish from Charlie. I'm glad he won't be coming over anymore, that he can't hurt her again, but I'm still worried about Mick.

'How's Mick gonna get home?' I say.

She takes another drag.

'He'll take the train instead. I've left a message for him.'

'The *Southern Aurora*?'

'I'm not sure that's running anymore.'

'The *Melbourne Express*?'

'Could be. But he should have enough for a ticket either way. I said for him to call if he hasn't.'

I'm pretty disappointed we can't pick him up, but part of me is relieved. With Charlie not around, things will be better. Mum can talk to Mick about Fernvale. We'll go to the bistro too, like last time. Like Mum promised. Just family.

He'll be excited about the deli, about the fresh start. And I'll tell him about *The Firefox* as well. I ask Mum if we can walk down and pick Mick up from the station.

'It'll be too late,' she says. 'He knows the way.'

•

I don't think Mick has ever been on the train from Sydney before. It'll be his first time. Mum said it's gonna leave from Central Station.

I've been to Central Station once, but it was ages ago. It was when Mum took me and Sam to the Sydney Easter Show one year. We didn't go on the *Southern Aurora* to get there, just a bus. I asked Mum if we could take Nan to the show, but she said it was too much trouble.

Central Station was enormous. It had huge brick arches like I'd never seen before, and there were people everywhere. There were tunnels underground too, with bright coloured tiles on the walls and the ceiling. It was amazing.

The Easter Show was pretty great as well. Way better than the carny. We went on the roller coaster, the pirate ship, and the dodgems. Mum even bought us a showbag each. Sam got the Bertie Beetle, which is mostly lollies and chocolates, and I got Batman.

I remember almost everything about that day. I remembered so I could tell Nan about it, Mick too. Nan was really happy for us, that we'd had such a good time.

'Sounds terrific, Jimmy,' she said.

I was happy when we were at the show, but sad at the same time. I was sad because Nan and Mick weren't there with us. Sad too because I didn't think we'd have another day like that for a long time, maybe never, and I wanted it to last.

Maybe we can go again, with Mick getting out. We can drive up there in the Pacer. It'll be great.

•

The *Melbourne Express* is meant to be really fast. Faster than the *Southern Aurora*. Definitely. That's what Danny told me.

But he said the *Southern Aurora* is better, with nicer carriages and better seats. It's all first class, so it must be better, even if it's slower.

He'd told me that back when we were still friends. I don't think we are anymore.

I try hard not to think about him and Chadwick, about what they're doing. I'm sure he's at Chadwick's, playing on the Amiga, or maybe swimming in his pool. I even thought about riding there and looking over the fence, to see if I could see them. But when I imagined it, seeing them together, it made me so upset that I changed my mind.

Later in the afternoon, me and Sam walk to the train station to find out exactly when the train is getting in. The walk takes my mind off things a bit.

'Mick's coming home tonight,' I say.

'Okay.'

'But it's gonna be late.'

'Yep.'

'Really late.'

'Yep.'

'It's good he's coming home, but I'm a bit worried.'

He squeezes my hand tight. It's sweaty and warm. He's got his Rubik's Cube in his other hand, and I can see he's fixed the green side.

'Maybe he'll be different this time. Maybe he won't get so angry. And it'll be better because Charlie won't be around anymore.'

'Okay.'

'You think so too?'

'Yep.'

'It's definitely good Charlie won't be around.'

'Okay.'

'Mum says they're finished, so now he won't hurt her anymore. He won't be mean to you, either.'

It feels good to say the words out loud. Like it makes it more real.

By the time we get back home, Mum is already cooking dinner. We have sausages in bread, with lettuce and tomato sauce. The lettuce is crunchy and the bread is soft and fresh. It's delicious.

Raiders of the Lost Ark is on the telly. Sam likes most movies, but especially ones with Harrison Ford. I get a cushion off the couch and put it on the floor for him, so he can sit up close. He likes to touch the screen sometimes, especially when Harrison Ford is on. I don't mind not seeing the whole screen, because I've seen it before at Danny's house.

I wonder if Danny is staying the night at Chadwick's. Probably. They're probably staying up late and watching videos. I try not to think about it, but it's hard.

Mum is sitting at the table in the kitchen. She's drinking the Kaiser and reading the newspaper. She must be thinking about Mick coming home, and the job in Fernvale with Aunty Pam.

But maybe the Kaiser helps her stop thinking about things, maybe it gives her a rest from worrying. Maybe it's good for that.

TWO

My alarm goes off at two-fifteen, and I turn it off quick. I stay in bed for a minute and listen to Sam's heavy breathing. I can tell he's sleeping deeply.

I get up as quietly as I can, so I don't wake him. In the green light from my alarm clock, I can see he's rolled on his side, his Rubik's Cube beside him. I put my jacket on over my pyjamas, then my shoes.

It's colder outside than I expected. My breath steams out in small clouds, and the Avenue is super quiet. Nearly all the lights are off, apart from the Party House. The Party House is where they have parties on most weekends, with fires out back in big steel drums. Mick used to go there with Travis Greenwood and Smelly, but then the police started turning up pretty regular.

It isn't too far to the train station from the Avenue. The railway line runs parallel to Richardson Street, so it's straight ahead from there.

There's houses on one side of Richardson Street, so I walk on the other side, where the cutting and the railway line is. There's no streetlights on that side, so I figure it'll be harder for anyone to see me if they drive past.

The grass is dry on the edge of the road, and it's noisy under my feet. A couple of hundred metres from the station, I see a car turn in from Macpherson Street.

I figure if it's anyone weird, I'll run for the station. I don't know if the station master will be there so late, but I hope so. Danny told me once that everything is automated now, so they don't need people to do the signals. Still, the train can't be too far away.

The car comes slowly up the street. I keep my eyes down and walk quickly, hoping they won't see me.

It pulls up on the opposite side, then does a U-turn, coming right up beside me. I hear the window squeal as it winds down, but I try not to look.

'Out a bit late, aren't you, mate?'

I take a deep breath in and out. I look across, and see it's a divvy van.

The copper turns off the engine. I can't see who it is, not exactly, especially from the passenger side. I know some of the coppers. A few different ones have come to our house to ask

Mick questions, usually when something bad has happened around town. Like they always thought it was him who did it.

'Bit too late for a young fella to be on his own, isn't it?' he says. 'Where's your mum?'

'Asleep.'

The copper turns on a torch and shines it at me, right in my eyes.

'Where you headed?'

'The train station.'

'Off to Melbourne then?'

'Picking up my brother.'

The copper turns off his torch.

'That right?'

'Yep.'

I think I can hear the train horn coming from a long way off, but I can't be sure.

'It isn't Mick you're going to meet, is it?'

I swallow. My throat hurts.

'Yep.'

'That's funny. The boss wants me to give Mick a bit of a welcome too. Make sure he feels at home.' He starts the engine. 'Why don't you get in?'

I can't imagine what Mick will do if he sees me with a copper, but I know it won't be good.

'Nah,' I say. 'I'm right.'

'You sure? I can drive you both home after too, like one big happy family. What do you think?'

'I'll walk. It isn't far.'

He turns on his headlights.

'Suit yourself. Can't say I didn't offer.'

•

There's no one working at the station, and I can't see the copper anywhere. I figure he must've changed his mind.

When the train arrives, it isn't the *Southern Aurora*. It's a pretty long one, with about ten carriages, but most of them look nearly empty. I'm not sure if it's the *Melbourne Express*, and there's no one I can ask.

It goes past the station like a snake, but eventually stops with the last two carriages in front of the platform. The windows are fogged up from the cold. For a minute, it looks like no one is going to get off. Maybe Mick missed the train. Or he was upset we didn't pick him up in Sydney, and he isn't coming at all.

The train horn sounds. It's about to take off again. The door of the last carriage swings open. A duffle bag flies out and lands on the platform with a thump.

Mick's hair is really short again, and he looks even skinnier than the last time. He has tight black jeans on, leather boots, and a woollen jacket. The woollen jacket was made at StormShield. I know because Mum got Mick a new one for Christmas and posted it to him, but it looks like he still has the old one on. Maybe he's saving the other one for special occasions.

The train toots its horn again. Mick picks up his bag and slings it over his shoulder. He eyes me. I'm not sure what to say.

'Jesus.' He grins. 'Look at you in your pyjamas. What a welcoming party.'

I smile. I can't help it.

The train slowly pulls away.

'Overshot the platform,' Mick says. Steam comes out of his mouth like he's a dragon. 'How long you been waiting?'

He drops the bag and pulls a pack of smokes from his jeans.

'Not long,' I say.

He lights one up. 'Mum?'

'Asleep.'

'She know you here?'

'Nah.'

'Sam's okay?'

'Yep.'

He takes a deep drag and lets out a thick plume of blue smoke.

'Better get moving then.'

'Yep.'

He picks up his bag, then puts his arm around my shoulders, which he's never done before. He sees my look, smiles, then slaps me on the back.

'Good to be home,' he says.

•

It turns out the copper did come. The divvy van is parked just outside the train station, over the street. Its lights are off.

I feel sick in my guts when I see it.

'Did you know he was there?' Mick says.

'Nah.'

'Say anything to you?'

'Nah.'

'You sure?'

'Yep.'

I don't like lying about it, but I don't want Mick to get fired up either. I just want to get home before there's any trouble.

The divvy van starts up.

'It's good to see you, Jimmy,' he says. 'Been too long.'

It's like he's pretending the divvy van isn't there, which is good.

It's gotten colder, and I'm shivering a bit. I zip up my jacket to my chin. The copper drives past slow, headlights still turned off. He turns the corner at Macpherson Street. A couple of minutes later, I hear the police siren in the distance, but then it stops. He must've pulled someone over.

Mick is quiet pretty much the whole way home. He doesn't say anything for ages. Then, when we get near the end of Richardson Street, he stops and lights another smoke.

'How's things been at home?'

'Okay.'

'Mum?'

I shrug. 'Good.'

He eyes me. 'Drinking much?'

'Sometimes.'

'She working?'

'Not really.'

'What about Charlie?'

'What about him?'

'Him and Mum still together?'

'Nah. She said they're finished.'

'Finished? Since when?'

'Just since yesterday, I think.'

He raises his eyebrows. 'Is it permanent?'

I shrug. 'Hope so.'

'Fair enough. Between you and me, he's a bit of a cunt.'

I wonder whether to tell him about Aunty Pam and Fernvale, about the job in the deli. But I decide it can wait. Mum should tell him, because she'll be able to say it better.

When we get near the top of the Avenue, he stops again and flicks his cigarette out into the street. The red embers spray, then disappear. He looks back up Richardson Street. There's no sign of the copper, or anyone else. It feels too quiet, so I try to think of something else to say.

'What was the train trip like?'

It's all I could think of.

He looks at me but doesn't say anything for a bit. He lights another smoke.

'Long and boring,' he says.

We keep walking. He puts his arm around me again. I try not to smile.

I can hear a few of the morning birds starting up early, and I know the sun won't be too far away. For a second, there on the street with no one else around, I close my eyes and let myself dream.

I dream that Mick won't get into any more trouble, and we'll definitely move to Fernvale. Mum will work in the deli. I'll make new friends, and everything will be better.

I open my eyes as we round the corner, and I know straight away that something is wrong. A feeling at first, but then I see.

Flashing blue and red lights.

The police.

And an ambulance.

THREE

Sometimes, if you let yourself dream of things getting better, they get worse. I should've known, but I'll remember for next time. I won't make that mistake ever again.

Mick paces the waiting room. Sam is asleep in a bed in one of the rooms in the emergency ward. We've just been in to see him, but only for a minute because the nurse said he needs to rest. He has a black eye, but they've done some tests and the doctor thinks he'll be okay. They say it's just bruising.

There's no one else in the waiting room, except a nurse behind the desk.

The police told Mick they're looking for Charlie, but Mick reckons he might've already shot through.

'The cops won't do shit,' he says.

When the sun starts to come up, the nurse behind the desk tells us we can go see Mum. But the doctor has to talk to us first. He's tall and thin, with steel-framed glasses. He talks in a whisper.

'She's heavily sedated,' he says. 'The CT of her brain has come back clear, but she's got some abdominal bleeding. You can see her just for a minute.'

When we get outside her room, the door is ajar. I feel scared. Scared about what I might see, how she might look.

I wish I was brave. I wish I'd stayed home to protect her and Sam. I shouldn't have snuck out like that.

But wishing for things doesn't change anything.

•

It's not like in the movies. There's no one else in her room, and there's just a machine going beep. It's connected to her arm. The machine has numbers on it, and I wonder what they mean. She has a mask on her face, which must be helping her breathe.

She looks asleep, with a white sheet and blanket pulled up to her chest. Her arm is in plaster, and her face is red and swollen. Through the mask, her nose looks much bigger than it was, with tape across the middle.

Her left eye is purple and red, and there's a lump like an egg on her forehead. I watch her chest going up and down. I try hard to be brave, but the tears come quick.

Mick squeezes my shoulder.

'Shhh,' he says. 'She's gonna be okay. You heard the doctor.'

'Did he break her arm?' I say.

Mick nods. 'Must've.'

His jaw flexes, and I can tell he's gritting his teeth. He shakes his head.

'That fucking cunt,' he says.

He says it softly to himself, but I hear.

There's a knock at the door, and the doctor comes in. The nurse from the waiting room follows, then stands beside him.

'I know it's a shock,' he says. 'But it looks much worse than it is.'

'Right,' Mick says.

But I can tell he's thinking about something else. He's thinking about Charlie. I can see it in his eyes.

'Best to leave her to rest now. We'll take good care of her.'

I wipe the tears from my cheeks. I go up beside the bed, then touch Mum's hand. I don't know if she can hear me or not, but I say it anyway.

'I'm so sorry, Mum.'

•

Mick is walking up and down in the lounge room, smoking one cigarette after another.

'Has he hit her before?' he says.

I nod.

'This bad?'

'Nah.'

'Has he ever hurt you?'

'Nah.'

'Sam?'

'Sometimes,' I say. 'But not as bad.'

He butts out his smoke in the ashtray. 'Fuck this. I can't just sit round here.'

He puts on his jacket.

'Where are you going?'

He doesn't answer.

'Can I come?'

He gives me a look. 'Get to school. I don't want anyone coming here looking for you.'

'Are you going to see Mum?'

He shakes his head. 'Maybe later.' He picks up the keys for the Pacer. 'I'm gonna go find that prick.'

FOUR

Before I go to school, I decide to wait for Sam's bus outside our house. Don won't know about Mum and Sam being hurt, and I feel like I should tell him. It means I'll probably miss my bus, but I can ride my bike to school instead.

But when Sam's bus pulls up, it isn't Don driving. It's Johnny Burton again. Don is meant to be back by now, and I wonder where he is.

Johnny's okay, but he isn't as patient as Don. He's always worried about the time. He pulls up to the gutter and opens the door.

'G'day, mate. Where's your little brother?'

'He's sick.'

'Fair enough.' He cuts the engine. 'You all right?'

'Yep,' I say. 'Where's Don?'

Johnny shakes his head.

'They treat me like a mushroom, mate.' He grins, and his teeth are all yellow. 'Still up north seeing his sister. Or off sick. One of them two.'

I nod.

'You sure you're all right?'

'Yeah.'

'You don't look all right.'

'I'm okay.'

'Well, I'd better get moving. Unless you want to jump on and spend the day with this lot.'

'When's Don getting back?' I say.

He shrugs.

'Dunno. But I'm off fishing next week, so he'd better be back by then.'

•

At school, I've been staying away from Danny and Chadwick. I don't want them to think I want to be friends again.

But I'm not really thinking about that so much anymore. I have other things on my mind. Bigger things.

I wonder if Mum's face will get back to normal, her arm too. He must've bashed her really bad for her to look like that. And I hope Sam's eye gets better quick, and that he's not too sore.

I'm worried about Mick too. If he's out looking for Charlie, the police might be following him. If he bashes Charlie, the police will arrest him and take him back to jail. Then it'll just be me and Sam on our own.

There's so many things that could go wrong, so I try to think of all of them. If I think of them, there's less chance of them happening. Or at least I'll be ready if they do.

It'd be better if I was with Mick. If I was with him, I wouldn't have to imagine all the things that could go wrong. Maybe I could even stop them from happening.

I spend recess in the library. I read *The Three Robbers*, which is one of my favourites. Danny always said it was meant for kids, and maybe that's true, but it's still excellent. It's a story about three robbers who steal from rich people, but then they kidnap a little girl who makes them change their ways. The pictures are scary, and the robbers have axes and incredible guns.

A few minutes before the bell goes, I head back to class. I want to get there early so I can get a seat near the back, as far away from Danny as I can get. Mrs Bon smiles at me when I leave.

'Bye, Mrs Bon,' I say.

'Goodbye, Jimmy.'

I've spent nearly every recess and lunch in the library since the race, and all we've ever said is hello and goodbye. Sometimes that's enough.

Out in the yard, someone calls my name. I know the voice straight away, but I pretend not to hear. He calls out again.

I turn and see him standing beside the toilets, near the back gate.

'What?'

'Come here for a sec.'

'Why?'

'Just a sec.'

'Where's Danny?'

I regret it as soon as I say it. I shouldn't have said anything. I should've pretended I didn't care.

'He's gone to the sports room.'

The sports room is where you can borrow equipment, balls and stuff. Mr Battista runs it.

'What do you want?' I say.

He stares at his feet.

'My mum wanted me to talk to you.'

'Your mum? Why?'

'It's just . . . I'm sorry. About what happened with Danny, I mean. Since the race.' He takes a deep breath. 'I know it wasn't your fault.'

It's nice he said it, but the race doesn't feel like it matters anymore.

'Mum thinks it'll blow over, but she said I should talk to you. She said I should apologise.'

'Okay.'

'She's really cross,' he says. 'She said I had to tell you that.'
I'm glad she's upset with him, but I don't say so.

'How's Sam?' he says.

I shrug. 'He's okay.'

We both go quiet. Part of me wishes I could tell him about Sam and Mum and Mick and Charlie, but it's too hard to explain. Before long, the music starts up for the end of recess.

'I'd better go,' he says. 'Danny will crack it if he sees me.'

'Yep.'

He looks like he's waiting for me to say something. Then, after a bit, he puts his hand out for me to shake it.

'I'm really sorry,' he says. 'I mean it.'

'Yep,' I say. 'Thanks.'

.

It wasn't something I'd planned. But if I was quick enough, I thought I could get back by the end of lunchtime. Easy.

When I get there, the garage door is closed. The Toyota Crown is in the driveway, but the curtains are drawn. I leave my bike in the front yard. I try the doorbell, then I knock.

There's no answer.

Maybe Johnny Burton was right. Maybe Don is still seeing his sister up north, even if he never mentioned that. I was sure he said he'd be back by now. And he definitely would've taken the Crown if he was going somewhere.

I hear a car coming up the street. I try to hide under the porch and press myself against the wall. You aren't sposed to leave school at lunchtime without permission. A red Celica goes past, but it's no one I know.

I pick up my bike in the yard. The sun is warm, but there's a cool breeze. A magpie calls from the powerlines out front.

I decide to look out back before I go. Maybe he's in the yard, or in the garage, and he didn't hear me. It wouldn't hurt to check.

I lean my bike against the fence, then go down the side. As I go past the Crown, I notice it's much dirtier than normal. There's mud around the tyres like it's been driven on a rough road, or maybe in a paddock.

'Don?' I call out. 'Are you home?'

There's no answer. I try the door to his garage, but it's locked.

'Don?'

'In here.'

I hear his voice coming from inside the house. I go round back and the kitchen door is ajar.

'Don?'

He's sitting at the table, and at first I don't realise what's wrong. Then I see his nose is swollen, his cheek bruised.

'Sorry I didn't get the door, mate. Haven't felt much like company.'

'Are you all right?' I say.

'Bit under the weather.' He forces a smile. 'But you should see the other bloke.'

'What happened?'

He shakes his head. 'Never mind that. But as you can see, the old snout isn't looking the best.'

I notice it's bent toward one side. And then I notice a Rubik's Cube on the kitchen table. The green side is done, just like Sam's.

I can't understand why it would be here in Don's kitchen, but it doesn't feel like the right time to ask.

'Do you want me to get some help?' I say.

He nods. 'Probably should get this seen to, but I'm feeling a bit too knackered to be driving right now. Maybe try Vince over the road, the Italian bloke. He should be able to give me a lift.'

·

Vince takes forever to answer the door. When he does, I realise why. He's an old man, even older than Don, with white hair combed back from his face. I hear music coming from inside, and a smell like nice cooking.

I tell him what happened.

'What's that?' he says.

'It's Don,' I say, louder this time. 'He's hurt.'

His eyes go wide. He goes past me and runs over the road, leaving his door wide open. Before long, he gets Don loaded up in his car.

Don looks at me and smiles. His nose looks terrible, a bit like Mum's. It must be broken. It was probably Charlie who did it, just like he did to Mum and Sam.

'Good stuff, Jimmy,' he says. 'Thanks for the help. And try not to worry. Your mum and Sam will be okay.'

'I get him to the doctor,' Vince says. He climbs into the driver's seat. 'You want a lift?'

I shake my head. How did Don know about Mum and Sam?

'I better get back to school,' I say.

I stand on the footpath with my bike and wait until Vince backs out of the driveway. He beeps the horn, and I wave.

●

I'm almost back at school when I see it. I hear it first, though, because there's only one car in town that sounds like that.

Mick looks at me, his eyes all dark and loose. A bit like when he used to go out all night with Smelly and Travis Greenwood. A bit like the time he bashed up Keith.

'Where are you headed?' he says.

I shrug.

'Well, you better get in then,' he says. 'I think we need to go for a drive.'

FIVE

My bike slides rough in the boot as Mick takes the corner. It's gonna get scratched, for sure.

'I called the hospital,' he says.

'Is Mum okay?'

'Yeah.'

'Is she awake?'

'Not yet.'

'We gonna go see her?'

'Later.'

'Sam?'

'He's fine.'

He lights a smoke, turns up the radio. It's the song about getting money for nothing, which I don't really like.

'Why aren't you at school?' he says.

I tell him about Don, about what I saw. About how I think Charlie did it. He doesn't say anything.

'Where are we going?'

He hocks something in his throat, spits it out the window.

'For a drive. Like I said.'

When we get to the edge of town he gets this funny look, like he's concentrating really hard. He turns the radio down.

He finishes his smoke and flicks it out the window. He suddenly looks much older than I remember. I notice the stubble on his chin, and dark rings under his eyes.

I wind my window down halfway, the air cool on my skin.

He takes a turn-off. It's the back road to the tip. It makes me think of Tippy. The day we rode out here, the day we buried him.

'Some things can't be undone.'

That's what Mick said.

He slows the car down and pulls up on the side of the road, but keeps the engine running. He lights another smoke and it feels much hotter inside.

I wonder if he caught up with Charlie. I wonder if he hurt him like he hurt Keith. I hope so. I hope he made Charlie pay for doing that to Mum and Sam, and to Don. Even so, I'm worried the police will get him for it.

My mouth is dry, and I try to swallow.

Mick takes a drag, blows the smoke out the window. 'I went to Charlie's cabin at The Meadows this morning. His shitty old Kingswood was there, but there was no sign of him. But I had an idea who to ask.'

'Who?'

'That dickhead Bluey. The one with the GT, out near Brownville.'

'Did he know where Charlie was?'

Mick shakes his head.

'He played dumb, so I fucked him up pretty bad. Smashed the windscreen of his GT and slashed the tyres too.'

He flicks his smoke out the window.

'Mum should've stayed away from Charlie.'

I know it isn't her fault, though. She was just lonely. She needed someone else, not just me and Sam. We weren't enough on our own, not without Mick. Not even with the Kaiser.

But I can't say so. It's my fault everything's gone wrong, not hers.

Mick turns the engine off.

'The cops will be all over me now, after what I did to Bluey.'

He stares straight ahead.

'Reckon I'll get out of town for a bit, Jimmy, keep a low profile.' He shakes his head. 'I'm not going back inside, no matter what.'

I wonder how bad he hurt Bluey. Maybe it's even worse than the time with Keith.

'Where will you go?'

He shrugs. 'Might head to Sydney, see a mate I met inside. But don't breathe a word to anyone.'

'Okay,' I say.

'You should come, you know? When you're old enough, I mean. When you finish school. There's nothing here, no future. And if you stay too long, you'll never leave. Or you'll end up like me.'

I can't imagine ever leaving Mittigunda on my own, not without Mum. Or moving to Sydney. The idea scares me.

'If you stay here, you'll always be from the Avenue. That's what people will say, no matter what you do.'

'What about Mum?' I say. 'And Sam?'

He shakes his head. 'I love Mum, and she didn't deserve what that prick did, but you can't depend on her. Sam will be okay. They'll look after him.'

But Mick doesn't know everything. He doesn't know about Fernvale, about Aunty Pam and the deli. About the fresh start. Things are going to get better.

So I tell him. I tell him about Don and about Aunty Pam so he'll know, so he might stay.

'She'll have a new job there,' I say. 'Things are gonna be different.'

He doesn't answer. We both go quiet, and it feels like ages before he says anything else.

'You know, I had this cellmate inside, an old bloke. He was a big reader, pain in the arse. Always had his head in a book, or giving bits of advice. One of the two.

'Annoyed the hell out of me at first, but he wore me down. Mainly because I realised a lot of what he said made sense.

'One thing he said, something that really stuck in my head, just before I got out. He shook my hand, and looked me in the eye. He said he hoped he'd never see me inside again, but there was something else he wanted me to remember. You know what he said?'

I shake my head.

'He said you should never believe what people tell you. But when someone shows you who they are, you should believe them.'

He starts the Pacer back up.

'The thing in Fernvale? The deli? It won't happen, Jimmy.' He turns on the radio. 'And even if it does, the booze will go with her.'

SIX

Mick stops the Pacer near the school gate, cuts the engine. He gets out and helps me get the bike out of the boot. It doesn't look like it was scratched, but that doesn't feel important anymore.

'Thanks for dropping me off,' I say.

'No dramas.'

He gets back behind the wheel, winds down the window.

'Remember what I said, right?'

'About what?'

He shakes his head. 'About keeping quiet.'

'Yep.'

He starts up the Pacer, gives it a rev.

'Don't end up like me, Jimmy. Whatever you do.'

I watch as he takes off down the street, engine rumbling. A few seconds later, a police car turns in from a side street. It follows the Pacer, and I wonder if Mick's spotted it too.

Bluey must've called the police, he must've told them what Mick did.

They turn on their flashing lights.

I hold my breath.

I wait for the indicator on the Pacer to start blinking, for Mick to pull over.

He doesn't.

He brakes and swings the Pacer around fast, its tyres screeching. The engine roars as it comes back toward me.

I try to catch Mick's gaze, to see if he might stop. But his eyes are on the rear-view as he passes.

The police car swings around and floors it, siren blaring.

Mick turns down another side street, disappears from view. The police car follows.

I hope Mick stops.

I hope he won't go back inside.

I stay there and listen until the siren fades into the distance.

I stay there until I can't hear anything else.

•

I'm halfway down the Avenue when I see him.

He's walking up the road, head down. White shirt and blue overalls. There's tape across his nose, a bit like Mum's.

'Jimmy,' Don says. 'Was just around at your place.'

'Yeah?'

'Yeah. I'm so sorry about your mum. Bloody terrible business.'

My heart beats hard in my chest.

'Is she okay?'

He nods. 'I saw her up at the hospital. Your Aunty Pam is with her and Sam now, and she'll be around to pick you up later. Must've been a hell of scare for you boys.'

'Yeah.'

'How come you're not at school?'

I shrug. 'Is your nose okay?'

'Ah, don't worry about me. Just a flesh wound.' He shades his eyes from the sun. 'Heading home then?'

'Yep.'

'Well, there's no one around there from what I could see. Why don't you come to my place for a bit, until your Aunty Pam comes by. We'll keep each other company.'

•

When we get to Don's, all the curtains are open. Warm sunlight fills the lounge room, the kitchen.

'We'll go out back,' he says.

As we walk through the kitchen, I notice a letter stuck to the fridge. It's from a hospital in Sydney, a place called St Vincent's, for an appointment with the Oncology Department. Maybe it's something to do with his sore back. I hope they can fix it.

Once we're out in the backyard, he tells me to sit.

'Had any lunch?' he says.

'Nah.'

I haven't had breakfast either, but I don't tell him.

'Righto. Let's see what I can rustle up.'

'I can help.'

'No, no. You're my guest.'

While Don's inside, I hear sirens in the distance. There's two different ones, the police and something else.

I hope Mick's okay.

After a few minutes, Don comes back out.

'You all right?' he says.

'Yep.'

He has a plate with two sandwiches. A ham one for me, salami for himself.

'Best I could do,' he says. 'Under the circumstances.'

I wolf mine down. He pushes the plate across with his second half.

'You have it,' he says.

'You sure?'

He nods. 'You're still growing.'

I take a bite and it's oily and spicy and delicious.

'How you been travelling?' he says.

I swallow the last of the sandwich. It's much better than the ham.

'Okay,' I say.

He leans back, puts his hands behind his head.

'You sure? Pretty rough time you've had.'

'I'm all right.'

A magpie lands on the patch of grass behind him, in the middle of the yard. It's a young one, its feathers a bit fluffy. An older magpie, maybe its mum, is perched up on the fence. The young magpie walks around, the mother watches.

'Mick's back now, isn't he?'

'Yep.'

'Must be good to see him after all this time.'

'I spose.'

He shakes his head. 'Bloody awful about your mum, though.'

'Yeah.'

'That Charlie's a real piece of work.'

'Yep.'

A blackbird lands down on the grass beside the magpie. It chirps. The mother swoops it. The blackbird chirps again, then flies up onto the fence. I hear another siren, different again. It stops pretty quick, though.

'Can I tell you something, Jimmy?'

I shrug.

'It's important, so I want you to really listen.'

'Okay.'

'It's something I want you to remember.'

He frowns, looks out at the backyard.

'You don't need to say everything's okay all the time. You don't have to pretend.'

The mother walks beside the young magpie. She tilts her head to the ground, then pokes her beak in.

'It's good to talk about things. About how you're feeling, I mean. I'm your mate, remember? Mates help each other out.'

The mother pulls out a worm. I wait for her to feed it to the young one, but she swallows it herself.

'How about I start. I'll tell you how I feel.'

Don clears his throat, crosses his arms, and looks up toward the sky.

'Things have been a bit rough for me lately. So I've decided to make some changes.'

The mother magpie finds another worm, the young one watches. The blackbird looks on from the fence.

'I'm gonna stop driving the bus, spend more time on things I enjoy. Maybe get the Austin up and running. See a bit more of my sister. Get to know my nieces and nephews a bit better.'

The young one tilts his head to the ground. The mother flies back up to the fence. The blackbird takes off.

'What do you think?'

'Sounds good.'

He smiles. 'It was you and Sam who inspired me. Working on *The Firefox*. Life's bloody short, you know?'

I nod.

'And I reckon I'll need help too, if you're still keen. With the Austin, I mean. How's that sound?'

'Good.'

The young magpie flies up to the fence beside the mother. Something passes between them, and they both take off.

'Your turn now.'

There's something in my chest. Something heavy. Right now, it feels as heavy and painful as it ever has.

So I tell him.

I tell him about Mick and Charlie and Bluey. About Mum and Brownville. About Danny and Chadwick. About Fernvale.

I tell him everything.

'It's all gone wrong,' I say. 'And it's all my fault.'

For a long time, Don doesn't say anything. A car passes out in the street. The clothesline creaks in the breeze. He reaches into his pocket, passes me a hanky.

'It's clean,' he says.

I wipe my cheeks.

'Should always have one with you. Comes in handy.'

I nod.

'I'm sorry,' I say.

'For what?'

'For getting upset.'

He shakes his head.

'I'm glad you told me.'

'What should I do?'

He sighs.

'Dunno, Jimmy. It's a tough one. You have to think things through. But you have to feel things too. What's in your heart, I mean, even if it hurts. That's the most important thing.'

He leans forward.

'But I want you to understand something.'

He clears his throat, and there's a whistle in his breath.

'Life is really unfair sometimes, but you can't control everything. You can't control what people think, or what they do. This world isn't perfect. Things always go wrong. Always. What you do matters, but it matters mostly for you. It's not your job to fix everyone else.'

I wipe my cheeks again.

'I know what it's like, you feel things really deep. I'm a bit the same. And you don't want others to feel it too. You don't want Sam or Mick or your mum to feel bad. But it isn't all up to you.'

I swallow. My throat hurts.

'You understand?'

'I think so.'

'Righto then,' he says. 'I reckon you've had enough of my sermons. For one day, at least.'

He smiles, squeezes my shoulder.

'How about we head over to your place to wait for your Aunty Pam. I reckon she'll be dead keen to see you.'

ONE YEAR LATER

There's a hill on the edge of town, but it's not as big as
Margaret's Hill. It has a bitumen road that's really steep,
and a dirt road out back.

We go up the dirt road, because it's always quieter that way,
especially after school. School is going okay, but I'm still the
new kid. I think it'll be like that for a while. Maybe forever.

I'm trying to make the best of it, though. Nan said once
that you need to make the best of things, even when they're
not perfect.

Sam only goes to school every second day, and Aunty Pam
looks after him when Mum's at work. It's good having Aunty
Pam around. She's like an extra mum. And it's nice when she

comes over, because her and Mum sit at the kitchen table and talk.

I like hearing their voices, even when I'm in my room and I can't hear exactly what they're saying. Just the sound of it.

•

Mick never made it to Sydney.

He only got as far as the highway, just outside of town.

The police said he lost control, that he was going too fast. But no one can say for sure.

There was an investigation into what happened, but Aunty Pam says it was rigged by the police, that they covered each other's backs.

She stayed with us for a while after Mick's crash, and helped me and Mum and Sam. Me and Sam didn't have to go to school for a few weeks, and Aunty Pam cooked us breakfast and lunch and dinner every day. She organised the funeral too.

Sam went quiet for a long time after Mick died. Quieter than the time with Nan. He wouldn't play with his Rubik's Cube either, even when Aunty Pam bought him a brand new one.

Mum stayed in bed for ages after she got out of hospital. She was just too sad to do anything. She did come to the funeral, though.

There weren't as many people as there were at Nan's funeral, maybe because Mick didn't live as long. There was just us and Don and Smelly, and Mrs Simpson from down the street. Mrs

Chadwick came too, even though she'd never met Mick. She sat right at the back.

It was the saddest day ever, even sadder than when Nan died, so I try not to think about it too much.

It's hard sometimes, though. I really miss him.

Maybe it'll be like that forever.

I've got Mick's Stephen King books in my room, *Salem's Lot* and *The Stand*. Aunty Pam told me I should have them, even if they're meant for adults, and even if they were actually Travis Greenwood's before he died.

I'm going to read them one day, definitely.

•

It was Mick who said some things can't be undone, and he was right about that. He wasn't right about everything, though.

We did end up moving to Fernvale, but it just took longer. We lived with Aunty Pam first, then Mum got us a flat. It's not as big as our house on the Avenue, or even Aunty Pam's place, but it's okay.

The job at the deli was gone by the time we came, but Aunty Pam helped Mum find another one. It's at the supermarket still, but not in the deli. She helps with stacking the shelves, and she says it's pretty good.

It took a long time for her injuries to heal from what Charlie did. The ones on the outside, I mean. Aunty Pam says she's still got some on the inside, mostly because of what happened to Mick, but also because of what Charlie did.

She still cries sometimes in her room. She does it with her little TV on, but I can hear her.

Mum hasn't had a boyfriend since, which is good, but she stays home a lot. Even more than before. She's still got the Kaiser too. It came with us, like Mick said, but I try not to check it as much. She needed the Kaiser every day for a bit, but not as much now.

Last thing Aunty Pam heard, the police still hadn't found Charlie. There's a rumour he changed his name, that he's working somewhere up north on a cattle station. But there's rumours too that someone killed him. She said Charlie had a gambling problem, and some big debts, and that someone might've caught up with him.

I wasn't meant to hear Aunty Pam say any of that, but I overheard her talking on the phone when we were still staying at her place. I don't know who she was talking to, though.

I haven't told anyone what I think. About what I'd wished for.

I remember Mick saying once that a mineshaft would be the perfect place to dump a body, but I don't know how he'd know.

And I'd never tell anyone that.

•

Me and Danny never became best friends again, but it got better. Chadwick helped. He invited me and Danny over to his place a couple of times when I was still in Mittigunda. I think it was probably Mrs Chadwick's idea, but he didn't say so. It didn't completely blow over like she said it would, but some of it did.

•

Don came to see us about six months ago. He didn't come in the Austin, though. He said he had to sell it to pay for a few things.

He came in his blue Toyota Crown instead. It isn't as nice as the Austin. Me and Sam helped him work on the Austin once his nose got better, before we moved town.

It was hard work, but good too. I really liked being in the garage with Don, with the radio on. It took my mind off things. We'd have lunch there most days when we worked, and it was almost always delicious. The salami especially. We had that more often, because I told him I liked it.

He was always patient with Sam, and always showed us how to do things more than once. It was annoying sometimes, how many times he'd show us, but I think he just wanted us to learn.

'So you'll know how to do it properly,' he'd say.

When he came to Fernvale, he looked different than before. He was all dressed up, in black pants and a white shirt. He looked much skinnier.

Mum made scones, and we sat at the table in the kitchen. Him and Mum talked and drank tea, and me and Sam had Milo. The scones were delicious, with cream and strawberry jam.

After a bit, Don told Mum he was leaving Mittigunda too. But he wasn't coming to Fernvale.

'Wollongong,' he said. 'To stay with my sister. Closer for treatment.'

Mum took a long time to say anything. Then she said it was a good idea, to spend time with family.

'It's what's important,' she said.

Don didn't stay for long, because he needed to get home before dark.

'Eyes aren't what they used to be,' he said.

But just before he left, he said he had a present for me and for Sam.

'Just something small.'

He went out to the Toyota Crown for a bit, then brought back two packages wrapped in newspaper.

'For all your work,' he said.

It was a box of hankies. White ones. In the corner of each was my initials, JM, in dark blue letters. He had the same for Sam too. SM.

'You like it, Sam?' he said.

Sam nodded.

'Thanks, Don,' I said.

He smiled. 'Always keep one with you, remember? Comes in handy.'

'Yep.'

When he was leaving, I asked when he was coming back. He looked at me for a long time before he answered. He looked at Mum for a second too, and then his eyes went all shiny.

'I'm not really sure, Jimmy. But I'll see you again, I reckon.'

I took Sam's hand and we walked back to the front step, but I could still hear Mum talking to Don. I stopped and turned to look at them.

'Have the police said anything?' she said.

'No.'

She touched his arm gently.

'If you hadn't come that night, that bastard would've killed us.' Her voice went all croaky. 'If Sam hadn't run to your house . . .'

Don shook his head. 'He'd had it coming for a long time, Nicki. And it was Sam who was the hero of the piece, not me.'

Mum gave him a big hug before he got back in the Crown. 'You're a good man,' she said. 'Good luck with everything.'

And when he started the car, Mum started crying. She tried to hide it, but I saw.

•

It's summer now, so there's extra time. More sunlight, and more time after school.

It takes longer going up the dirt road than up the bitumen one, but I prefer it. Sam doesn't complain, because there's more to look at. More trees, more birds. We even saw a whole mob of kangaroos once. Sam loved that.

At the very top of the hill, there's a rotunda. A rotunda is a round building with no walls that you see in parks sometimes, but this one was built as a war memorial. From up there, you can see out over the town and all the way to the hills.

We went up there for a school excursion a few months back, to learn about the war, but I was mostly interested in the view. There's even a coin-operated telescope, but it doesn't work very well.

From up there you can see all the paddocks and all the farms. It's like a patchwork on a blanket. It all looks so far away, but close at the same time. Like the whole world is right there, and you could reach out and take it in your hands. I like how peaceful and quiet it is.

At the top, where the rotunda is, it's all sealed and bitumen. It's where the proper road begins. The road that takes you back down.

I look at Sam.

'You ready?' I say.

'Yep.'

He sits down carefully, and I put the rope in his hands. It took him a while to learn how to steer, but we've had plenty of practice.

The seat is calf leather. Don got it made especially for us. He had a mate who made saddles for horses, and he did it for him as a favour. They were in the army together, he said.

The leather is light brown and incredibly soft. It's almost like sitting in a glove. It has white stitching all through it, and it's embroidered at the back.

It has our initials too, just like our hankies, in each of the top corners. Then the name in big gold letters.

The Firefox.

'You sure you're ready?'

Sam grips the rope tight.

We never caught the *Southern Aurora*, and Aunty Pam told us it doesn't run anymore. But she told me what it means. She said it's named after something you can see in the sky at night, when something bursts from the sun and makes coloured lights. She said it's very rare and you can only see it at certain times of the year, and only from certain places. It sounds pretty incredible.

I take hold of the bar at the back, the timber oily and smooth in my hands. We gain speed, the cool air rushing past.

The cart tilts downhill, and I close my eyes. I close my eyes and I think of Mick. He's in the Pacer on his way to Sydney, to see his mate. The sun is shining, the radio's on. He's almost there.

I think of Don in his backyard, and what he told me. I think of the world out there, just like a patchwork.

I breathe hard and deep into my lungs, and I run as fast as I can. I try to imagine the southern aurora. I try to imagine what it looks like, with bright colours bursting out from the sun.

And I do what Don told me, what he said I need to do.

I let go.

ACKNOWLEDGEMENTS

There are a number of talented people who help bring my books into the world. Special thanks to Vanessa Radnidge for her wisdom and friendship – you always know what I want to say, and how better to say it. I'm also deeply grateful to Stacey Clair, Deonie Fiford, and Sarina Rowell – thank you for your intelligence, insight, and for lifting my work into a higher realm.

Heartfelt thanks to my agent, Gaby Naher, and to Grace Heifetz – both of whom provided invaluable feedback (and tough love when needed). Thanks also to those fellow writers who read this story in its raw-boned early days, especially Melissa Manning and Janine Mikosza.

I am very grateful to Louise Stark, Fiona Hazard, and the entire team at Hachette Australia – I couldn't wish for a better publisher. Deepest thanks also to the booksellers who support my work and Australian writing more broadly. Without your passion and commitment, our country would be a poorer place.

This novel was written with support from the Australia Council for the Arts and Creative Victoria. It is a precious gift to have time to write, and one too few authors receive. It is vital that arts organisations are adequately funded to assist writers and other artists into the future.

I'd also like to pay special tribute to my mum, and my late father. My brothers and I were fortunate to have parents who were unfailingly brave, selfless, and who saw the value of education.

Lastly, my love to Georgia and Millie. Without you, none of this is possible.

LOVED *SOUTHERN AURORA*? READ ON FOR AN EXTRACT FROM MARK BRANDI'S GRIPPING NOVEL *THE OTHERS* . . .

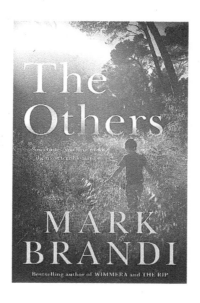

On his eleventh birthday, Jacob's father gives him a diary. To write about things that happen. About what he and his father do on their farm. About the sheep, the crop, the fox and the dam. But Jacob knows some things should not be written down. Some things should not be remembered.

The only things he knows for sure are what his father has taught him.

Sheltered, protected, isolated.

But who is his father protecting him from? And how far will his father go to keep the world at bay?

All too soon, Jacob will learn that, sometimes, people do the most terrible things.

don't think of you much anymore.

No one really knows about you. Only Sam, and she can't tell anyone. I don't have many friends. Don't need them. You taught me that.

Even if I did have friends, I couldn't tell them.

Good thing is, people around here don't ask too many questions. And what they don't know, they make up, which is fine by me. Plus, the rent's cheap.

The reminders are less frequent nowadays, less keenly felt. More often, if I'm honest, I'm searching for the feeling. Just to feel something.

It's as though if I don't feel it anymore, it isn't real. Sometimes I tell myself that's true.

But then, other times, it comes from nowhere. Like something sticking in my guts. Even after all these years.

It took me a long time to realise what happened, even if I've never really understood. When I was a kid, I thought everything would be okay. That you might come back and make things all right again. That they might help you, and you'd get better too. I didn't realise what I was feeling was grief. Sam's helped with that. Before therapy, I didn't know I was allowed to feel that sorrow. For what I lost, and for what I never had.

Didn't know I was allowed to, because of the things you did. The things I found out.

I also felt guilt. Guilt about what happened. But that's getting better.

Or it was. Until last night. And then today.

Last night I read a news story – it was a similar case, but not the same. They're never exactly the same. And only sometimes do I get a mention. Just for a local angle, I guess.

Has similarities to . . .

Reminiscent of . . .

Like the infamous . . .

I read the article. Read it again. Searched for other reports. I only had a minute before I had to get back on my shift. I do night shifts, mostly. Better money, less talk.

It wasn't the same. None could ever be the same as us.

What you did.

What I did too.

•

I woke up and had a feeling – a feeling of you being near.

When I shut my eyes, I could almost see you.

Your gold tooth.

Can't remember exactly what you look like anymore. And you'd be different now anyway, if you're still out there.

You're a spectre, drifting into my thoughts without a proper invite, then out again. Less of a trace, less form, with each passing year.

I can't remember everything, but I remember some things pretty clear.

Your anger.

The soft eyes, too.

But the *feeling* is something different. And the feeling is something I'm less able to get hold of. Can't conjure it – just comes unexpectedly.

And it wasn't the news story that did it so much.

Was something else.

And then, I saw it.

•

There's a gum tree in my backyard. A big one. When the wind's up, it creaks and cracks like it might be about to fall. Has done for ages.

My neighbour would love to see it gone. More likely to fall on me, not him. Unfortunately.

I like to look at it. I like to watch its branches in the breeze, and I look for subtle changes. The loss of bark, the beginning of a wattlebird's nest, a new sprout – all these things, I notice. You taught me to notice. You taught me on our walks.

I was drinking a coffee in the kitchen, looking out. I've always needed those moments, the quiet. More so lately.

I watched the tree, the gentle sway of its branches, the grey sky behind. And I could sense something. Something different, but I wasn't sure what.

I looked it up and down a few times, and something wasn't quite right.

And I felt it.

I felt it before I saw.

It was a broken branch – a small one, stood up between two of the larger roots, leaning against the trunk.

The sort of thing no one else would notice.

But I noticed. I noticed, because I watch that tree. And because I'm careful, like you taught me.

I knew it was a message.

I didn't finish my coffee. I went out there, into the cool of the morning. I picked up the branch, studied it. There was nothing to be read from its leaves, its smooth skin.

I placed it on the ground.

I didn't want anyone else to notice, didn't want them to see what I saw.

But no one else would see, or understand – that's the whole point.

Only me and you. We're the only ones who'd know.

The only ones who knew.

And I know you might come for me.

Because I had to choose.

Because I'm one of the others.

·

You taught me a lot when I was young, a lot of things that made me who I am. Like keeping a diary – you said that would help. It'd help my writing, you said, and help keep my thoughts in order.

I've still got the old diaries, but I never look at them.

It wouldn't hurt to look now. I know what happened, of course. Most of it, at least. The facts, I mean, not the feelings.

The feelings I've kept out.

Had to.

But I remember some of the things you said.

I remember one thing you said, especially, more than once.

If the others come, everything will change.

You were wrong about a lot of things. Most things, really. But you were right about that.

Sam reckons I should read them. She says to understand ourselves in the present, we need the context of our past. We need to attach meaning.

'It's no good just repressing our feelings.'

That's what she tells me.

But she doesn't know everything. Everything that happened, I mean. No one knows that.

Only me and you.

If she knew everything, she might think it's better not to look back.

Because sometimes, things are better left in the past. Dangerous things. Things like you.

The branch against the gum tree is a message. I know it. I know you're watching. And now the past is here.

So I need to look back and remember what you told me, what you did.

I have to remember all about you.

I have to remember, so I'm ready.

So I'm ready if you're coming.

I'll get the rifle out too. Just in case.

In case you're coming.

Just in case you're coming for me.

ALSO BY MARK BRANDI

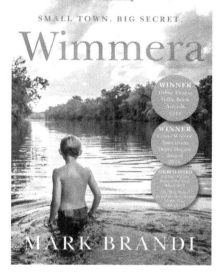

'a languid, unsettling novel that perfectly captures life in small-town Australia ... literary crime fiction at its best'
Books+Publishing

SMALL TOWN. BIG SECRET.

Wimmera

WINNER
Debut Fiction
Indie Book
Awards
2017

WINNER
Crime Writers
Association
Debut Dagger
Award
2016

SHORTLISTED

MARK BRANDI

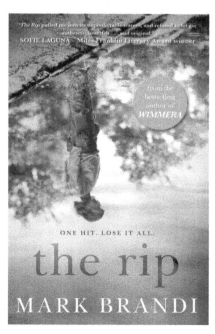

'*The Rip* pulled me into its unpredictable waters, and refused to let go; authentic, heartfelt ... and original'
SOFIE LAGUNA – Miles Franklin Literary Award winner

from the bestselling author of *WIMMERA*

ONE HIT. LOSE IT ALL.

the rip

MARK BRANDI

hachette
AUSTRALIA

If you would like to find out more about Hachette Australia, our authors, upcoming events and new releases, you can visit our website or our social media channels:

hachette.com.au

 HachetteAustralia

 HachetteAus